Smoke From The

A Story

John Arthur Cooper.

Incorporating the short story

'The Gun.'

Chapter 1.

Reginald Moorcroft set out to work. The white aluminium double glazed frosted glass front door clunked familiarly shut. The silver Honda Civic beeped obediently as it responded to the key fob. He glanced at the two door mirrors as the car glided backwards out of his wooden gate. The gaps were OK. He'd done it a thousand and one times but he always glanced.

'Today I'm wearing light brown leather lace up Hush Puppy shoes. Matching beige plain Marks and Spencer socks. Fawn twill trousers, thirty eight inch waist with a plain mid brown leather belt with dull brass buckle. In my left trouser pocket is my mobile phone; Nokia of course! And a white handkerchief ironed by Rosamund into a triangle. In my right pocket another hanky, a pen and an unknown amount of loose change. There's nothing in my back pockets as it hurts my arse when I sit down. I spend a good portion of my life sitting down.' His thoughts meandered off track. 'My shirt is also Marks and Spencers. A tasteful light blue striped with white beige and black thin lined pattern. My wife Rosamund has just turned the collar for me as it was beginning to fray. Tie? A plain silk grey, tied in a single Windsor knot. It's June so I'm not wearing a vest. If I do wear a vest I wear the sleeveless 'Onslow' type when it's not too cold but if it's very cold I wear a white T shirt type with a round or sometimes a V neck. It depends what I get from my daughters at Christmas. I've got a thin greenish orangey pullover on today as there's a bit of a cold wind. My coat is a tan shower-proof long jacket I got in a sale at a shop in Birmingham. I didn't intend to buy it. I had to go to court one day and was wandering around during a long lunch break when I spotted it in a sale down from a hundred and seventy eight to ninety. It was such good quality and reversible, the other colour is black so I tend to always go for the tan. I've had it three years and wear it most days for work. In the right hand inner breast pocket is my wallet. Black and folded, Thirty quid, debit card, credit card, organ donor card, work identity card, a car park entry swipe card to the Police Station front yard, two paper clips, a ten euro note from last year's holiday in France. A couple of business cards, an old SIM card and a small piece of paper with key telephone numbers on in case I lose my phone. Sadly! No condoms! In my right hand coat pocket is a small blue and grey multi tool with a built in Pea light. I don't know how the light works but it never seems to run out, various old car park tickets, a biro and another hanky. In my left is a folded and crumpled pamphlet for English Heritage.'

His mental meanderings were disturbed by the need to turn his car left at the 'T' junction. The disturbing indicator noise self canceled allowing him to settle back into his thoughts.

'My car is 'X' reg and seven years old. I should get a new one but this does everything I want with very little complaint. Tyres and that's about it. Oh I did have to have a nearside front suspension bush changed for last year's MOT. We've never had any kids. Rosamund uses her blue beetle so the inside of my car gets very little use or abuse. It's black and clean. The closest it gets to litter is the odd McDonalds bag which I always bring home, then I know it's properly recycled. The driver's footwell is the only area that shows any sign of use. I usually hoover that out once a week after I've put it through the car wash. Yes I know car washes are supposed to scratch your car but it's silver and doesn't show them up, plus I'm not inclined to use one of those East European hand car washes that sprout up on every bit of roadside space with a reachable water supply. My radio is always on Radio two. Sometimes if I'm feeling serious I switch to Radio four but mainly it's two. I can't stand local radio, the DJ's, presenters, call them what you will, are so amateurish and the constant repetitive adverts drive me nuts. It's got air conditioning but all I use it for in UK is an express demister when it's very wet and everything mists up. We use it on holiday of course. You have to. Hours of drumming down the Route De Soleil is just intolerably noisy with the windows open so we use the air con then but you can see it on the petrol consumption. It's automatic. I got bored and tired of changing gears years ago and my daily commute sees me crawling through Hereford's rush hour twice a day. To be honest you can't really do any journey of any length without running into some sort of jam or queue. So it's a godsend! One foot and steering is about enough. It's so mind numbingly tedious.'

Reg rolled to a slow and easy halt at the pelican crossing. A teacher shepherded about twenty five children across. They looked about six years old. She looked about forty two, no make up, unfashionable frizzy hair half grey, half black, wearing beige slacks and a navy blue nylon puffa jacket. Each compartment of the jacket struggled to escape. He wondered what colour knickers a woman like that would wear. Definitely not a thong. He decided they would be white. Had a woman like that ever had oral sex? Had she ever been so passionate and out of control as to guide a man's hard wet cock into her wet sucking mouth. He looked at her mouth. It was small and pinched. He decided it wasn't big enough to get a decent cock in. Was that the key to a woman's sexuality? Were all smiling happy women with broad wide mouths up for a blow job? He decided he would take note of women's mouths and pursue the theory. The issue of blow jobs with Rosamund had never been on the agenda.

BEEP! BEEP! The insistent noise jolted him back to reality. Glancing into his rearview he could see a yellow transit inches from his bumper. He took his foot off the brake and the car cruised slowly forward under the power of the idling engine.
'Keep your hair on! None of us are going anywhere fast' he thought.

He'd been a 'crime analyst' at the Police Station for the last eighteen years. It was easy and comfortable. Algorithms did all the legwork. Automated reasoning had now replaced the filing cabinet. Intuition was now computerized. Hunches held no sway. Those years had seen his hair retreat to the sides of his head. His carefully packed lunches deposit themselves around his midriff. His hazel eyes now assisted by glasses. His sexuality diminished by complacent harmony and a peaceful home. All he did was pick out information from a screen and frame it in a way that young keen police officers could read on A4 size posters that decorated parade rooms throughout the force or compile actions for work overloaded detectives to complete. Occasionally his local knowledge and experience led him to a different conclusion than the computer but not often. The machine was getting cleverer and better. He was getting older. His mental meanderings always took him back to the same basis. It was just maths based on one thing "people don't change" or at least if they did it was very slowly. Given the same circumstances, the same conditions, the same opportunities, people will always make the same decisions and do the same things. Computers just ruthlessly exploited this fact. He often thought things like this through whilst supposedly beavering away in front of his green screen. He reckoned that within his lifetime society would divide. Life was so recorded and accountable that only criminals would use cash. The great washed majority would sacrifice their privacy for a perceived convenience.

"Morning Reg. Bit nippy today."

Thom Fairfax, a DC half shouted to him as he waited for the barrier to open. The open window let in the brisk breeze.

"Morning Thom. Any good on the lottery this weekend?"

"No. Nothing. You can't throw the computer out of the window and retire just yet Reg!" Thom laughed.

"I don't know why I bother with that bloody syndicate; all I've had is twenty quid in ten years!"

"Yeah! Same here but we both know that if we pull out that's the week it'll hit the jackpot, then you and I'll be suicidal!"

"You don't have to be right all the time Thom. Give me a break will you?" Reg laughed as the driver's window slid shut.

Reg grabbed his black leather briefcase from off the back seat and launched himself out of his car. He couldn't remember when it had started to take conscious effort to get out of his car but it did now. A brief walk under the tunnel and a right turn took him to the rear door of the police station. The thirty second trek took him past the steel encased ramp that led to the charge room. A scruffy unkempt dirty youth was bouncing down the ramp having just been ejected from the charge room. A pink paper in one hand and a fag in the other. His alcohol induced actions from the previous night hiding behind his cocky noisy exit. Reg punched in the ever changing code to the back door, turned the handle to the left and pulled gently. He didn't pull confidently as he hadn't heard the usual mechanical click that indicated the code's acceptance. Sure enough the door remained locked and closed. Reg reached for his mobile phone but before he started to call up his office a young fresh faced Probationary Constable walked up. Reg didn't know him so he stood to one side as the boy in a uniform gave him access.

'Lift or stairs?' He thought. He caught sight of himself in the mirror-like metal finish of the lift doors. 'Stairs!'

By the time he'd made the third floor several young fit PC's had passed him. Either flying down clutching a file of papers. Their functional jackets, handcuffs, batons, radios, mobile phones, CS spray pouches all jangling in unison. Or galloping upwards two steps at a time. Serious young men. Smart and polished with short hair and sharp features. The last two flights of stairs caused Reg to assist himself by pulling on the handrail with his right hand.

"Morning Reg, good weekend?" Corrallee chirped at him. Corrallee was the office manager. Crisp, quick and intelligent, she was married to Dereck, an old fashioned CID officer who had now retired and had, in effect, stayed in the same job as a civilian statement taker.

"Oh you know! The usual! Endless demanding sex on the Oriental Express as it sped across the Russian Steppes towards China then a spot of wild goat hunting to extract musk and sell it at a huge profit in Hong Kong."

"You cut the lawn and washed the car then?"

"Yes."

The large office was crowded with desks adorned by women. Not pretty sexy women but functional practical Hereford women. Things got done efficiently and mainly on time.

His journey through the grey tough tiled carpeted office was just a series of hello's, mornings, and good morning's depending on how well he knew each person. They were always changing. He surmised that was one of the two things you could rely on in life, that nothing would stay the same for long. The other was death.

He unlocked his office and entered. Took off his coat and hung it on the rack of four pegs affixed to the wall behind the door. He put his briefcase down to the left of his chair. The walls were painted magnolia, the grey aluminium inoperable windows viewed out onto Blue School Street. The ceiling was mottled with whitish polystyrene panels, held and constrained by grey aluminium strips, only interrupted by double barreled white bright light fluorescents. He sat down at his desk and looked at his blank lifeless computer.
It was a grey day outside; his computer was sort of light beige grey. The carpet tiles were light grey. For fucks sake! His hair was grey, that is what little hair he had was grey. He glanced at his tan coat hanging on the hook. He decided he needed some colour in his office. Some reds and yellows.

Glennys entered his office without knocking and placed a plain white mug of hot dark instant coffee onto the West Mercia Constabulary coaster on his desk.

"Morning Reg. Good Weekend?"
'Well if you consider that I didn't die in a terrible car crash or was not maimed for life by a drug crazed terrorist trying to assassinate my pet hamster. Yes."
"I never had you down for a hamster man." Said Glennys.
"Ahhh. There's an awful lot you don't know about me, Glennys."
"How about you? Do anything Exciting?"
"Yep? Went for a long walk with my husband and the two dogs on windswept Garway Hill. Really enjoyed it."
"Can you tell the difference between them?"
"Oh yes, Betty has a white patch on the side of her head and Irene hasn't."
"No, I mean between your husband and the dogs?"
Glennys glared down her nose at Reg then flounced out in mock anger.
'She's beginning to look like an Old English sheepdog herself.' Thought Reg. He thought again then got up and followed her out to her desk in the main office. Taking a ten pound note out of his wallet he gave it to her.
"When you go out at break time will you get me some flowers? I fancy something yellow and red in my office."
Glennys looked up at him in a pained strange questioning way but by now Reg had turned and was on his way back.
His desk was tidy. He had nothing to put on it. All he did was direct electronic traffic, sometimes he added to it but mostly he just re-directed it.
'Oh well, here we go.' The green screen burst into life with awkward stilted text.

Ten thirty saw Glennys and his second cup of coffee. He used to go up to the canteen for the morning break but found it too stressful. He knew most people but all in different ways and to different degrees. He found having to grade responses tiresome. Then there were the slot machines. Totally unfathomable to him. The myriad flashing fluttering lights that leapt around a confusing display just seemed so pointless. The accomplished, pressed, nudged, looked and sometimes collected from them. It always seemed that the super confident, the larger than life egos, the really popular people were the ones that stood forever in front of the beeping cascading monsters. He was worried that if he sat on his own, which he preferred, he would be cast as a lone weirdo; he had to sit at a table with someone or some people. This necessitated some sort of meaningless random conversation. Other people just did it, they didn't seem to have a problem with it but he had to actively think of things to say. It was hard work. He had become a semi recluse in his magnolia office.

Glennys plonked the bunch of pink carnations and yellow roses on his desk along with seventy five pence change.
"What do I put them in Glennys?" Asked Reg.
"I've no idea. All you asked for was yellow and red flowers."
"Is there anything in the main office?"
"No! It's not a hospital. It's an office in the Police Station. Use the waste paper bin."
Reg looked at the rarely used clean grey new bin.
"It's grey. I can't use that."
"I've got a Glen Fiddich whisky bottle tin case in the bottom drawer of my desk. Someone gave me and George a bottle for Christmas."
"What colour is it?"
Glennys looked disparagingly at him.
"Dark red."
"That'll do. Be a love, pop some water in it for me will you?"
Glennys glowered and flounced out again. Five minutes later she returned and deposited the wet tall red can on his desk. Without speaking she left. He knew she suspected he was getting strange in his dotage.
Reg released the flowers from their elastic band and placed them into the tin. He didn't even try to arrange them. A simple flourish and they were on his plain window sill. They were yellow and red amongst the magnolia and grey. He turned back to his screen.

Eleven Thirty, time for the toilet. Leaving his office he locked the door and turned right heading for the mahogany coloured wooden door at the end of the long outer office. None of the office women spoke to him but he could imagine them thinking 'There goes Reg for his eleven thirty piss'.

Out in the corridor the walls changed from smooth magnolia to rough textured cream. The entrance to the toilet was simply a gap in the wall. You entered and turned right to be faced with a simple push sprung wooden door with a light grey aluminium push plate. There was no knob or handle to operate. Reg pushed the door open with his right shoulder. After all these years, all this familiarity, toilets were still stressful places. Once again it was the conversation that was the problem. What do you say to someone standing next to you with your dick out? 'What do you think of the current crisis in Ethiopia?' seems a bit on the heavy side. Whereas 'I see you've got some new tyres on the old Astra' seems too domestic by half. No, it had to be thought out and prepared for a whole range of people, ego's and circumstances. Where do you stand? If it's crowded and there's only one pistol left that's OK but if there's only three people in and they've occupied pistols one, three and five, where do you go? Which 'couple' do you join? He considered always going into a cubicle but that was suspicious. People would wonder? Has he got a tiddler? Has he got a python? No it had to be the pistols.

As he entered he could see the only person in the smelly room was Bert McCafferty. Bert was a comfortable, pleasant PC about to retire and move back to Ireland to take over the family farm.

"Hello Bert how's it going?" Reg asked. Bert was just at the end of his urinating, just starting to shake his dick quite violently prior to zipping up.
"Hi Reg OK thanks. Be a lot better at two o'clock though. God I hate early's. Getting up at four thirty on a cold dark morning has somehow lost its attraction after twenty nine years."
"You should have gone for promotion like the rest of the nine to fivers."
"I should have done a lot of things Reg but here I am about to collect a PC's Pension."
Bert had now moved over to the row of sinks and was half heartedly washing his hands.
"What about you? You can't have long to do?"
"I'm here for the duration. I think I'll die in my magnolia office. The only thing that worries me is that no one will notice that I'm dead."
"Oh they will. Glennys will notice your coffee has gone cold." Reg and Bert chuckled as Bert left the toilet.

Reg washed his hands and looked at himself in the mirror. 'Mr. Mundane, that's who you are. Mr. Average. Mr. Boring. Mr. Safe. Mr Mondeo Man except I've got a Honda civic. But! He thought further. I even find extreme sports boring. The thought of whizzing around doing things where the probability of getting seriously hurt was high, just seemed ridiculous. And for what. There's always somebody faster tomorrow. Football, Cricket, Rugby, even the Olympic Games were tedious. Fame for an instant! No thanks,' he thought. His aversion to any sport put him well outside the usual blokes clubs of 'did you see the match? Did you see the game? That was a good result on Saturday.'
Reg fumbled in his right pocket for his car keys and opened his office. Sat down, finished his now lukewarm coffee in one gulp and tapped in his password. The green lines of text sprang to life forcing him to scan and redirect the electronic traffic. He glanced over at the flowers. They looked alien and lovely. The warmth of the office already causing them to relax and open.
'They'll be dead and brown in four days' time then you'll have wasted a tenner.' His pragmatic gremlin bit him on the ankle.

Glennys popped her head around the door at precisely one o'clock.
"I'm off now Reg. If you remember I've got this afternoon off to go and see my mum at the hospice."
Reg turned away from the screen and looked over his glasses.

"Who's getting my afternoon coffee?"
Glennys huffed indignantly down her nose.
"Karen."
"OK See you tomorrow."
Glennys slammed the door.

Reg reached down for his briefcase and clicked it open inside was the Guardian Newspaper and his Tupperware lunch box. Prizing the lid from the base revealed two ham, tomato and lettuce sandwiches cut triangularly and made with wholemeal bread. He insisted on Lurpak butter even though Rosamund was constantly trying to wean him onto some low cholesterol spread. The ham was Duchy of Cornwall organic from Waitrose; a thin smear of Colman's mustard finished it off. Today it was an apple for afters. Tomorrow it would be a plain yoghurt. He needed a long drink after the dryness of the wholemeal bread. A bottle of elderflower cordial from Marks did the trick. It cost him four pounds twenty five for a week. Glennys always got one of the young office girls to pick them up on a Monday. By one fifteen he was finished. The Tupperware back in his briefcase. He would lock his door, take his shoes off and read the paper. It was a little left wing but at least it wasn't a comic. Thursdays was best. It was near the end of the week and the social supplement was always quite interesting. Sometimes he would nod off for ten minutes.

It was five past two Karen clicked open the door and entered with his coffee. Karen was about twenty five or six, engaged to be married to one of the PC's and hopelessly in love.
No matter from what remote angle a conversation started it would always end up with 'Adrian thinks! Adrian says! Adrian always! Adrian did! Adrian didn't!' She considered the Guardian as some insidious academic left wing rag. She called it 'Reg's Taliban Times'
"Put your 'Taliban Times' away Reg, here's your coffee, now get some work done!"
"Yes Miss! Very nice blouse today!" He really thought 'lovely tits' he imagined them constrained within a cream lacey bra, spilling out at the side. Heavy and fluid.
She knew his lewd connotations and left his office knowing and quite pleased he was looking at her bottom.

The cream and green machine dragged him back. He was important. Many criminals were in prison because of him and his tame algorithms. Many people had not been frightened or attacked because of him. No one noticed prevention. Not many people noticed him!

At three thirty he stood up and stretched. He'd had four phone calls that afternoon. An inquiry about a gang from Cardiff. One about a series of bizarre sexual murders in Gloucestershire. A strange one from Ross-on-Wye about a man who may have killed and disposed of his daughter many years ago and an inquiry from Birmingham about some ram raiders who always stole and used Subaru Imprezas. He looked out at the silently moving traffic as it paraded past his flowers.

Karen brought in his coffee, said nothing and left.

At five past five he put on his coat, locked his office and headed down the wide dappled stairs. Most people seemed to naturally gravitate towards 'on the right for down' and 'on the right for up'. Very few people walked up the middle that is unless they were walking together and even then the stronger personality usually took a lead position. There were no notices telling you to do it. It just happened.

The lift doors hissed and pinged open just as he got to the ground floor. Karen and Brenda spilled out into the lobby. Brenda was as wide as she was tall. Her tits were in competition with her stomach as to which stuck out the most.
"Eight minutes past five. Bit early for you Reg isn't it? It's usually nine minutes past!"

"Light traffic on the stairs so I thought I'd live dangerously. You know, move into the fast lane for a while."

"Does Rosamund know?"

"No! I move so fast she can't see me. Faster than a speeding bullet!"

"Show us your red underpants then Reg?" Karen giggled.

"Can't. I usually do it spinning round in a phone box."

"Better tell the Police! We've finally found who keeps leaving sticky messes in phone boxes." Brenda piped up.

"Goodbye Ladies!" Reg moved out of the clunky door and into the yard leaving the giggling pair behind.

He inched the Civic slowly forward behind Stuart Williams in his beige cavalier and Sally Richards in her white mini metro. The yellow and black bar swung mesmerizingly up and down as the cars made a break for freedom. Go! Go! Go! The radio two drive-time sports slot came on so he hit the radio four button. The whole of Hereford was inch crunchingly grid locked as bizarre individual thoughts, worries, dreams and aspirations bounced around inside each tin car. Unable to get out. Thank goodness. He couldn't think of anything more tedious than to have to communicate whilst commuting.

The grey evening made red rear brake lights seem glaring and aggressive. The city limits were reached barely touching the throttle, just inching forward with the engine idling. Then it was there. The open road. The Civic leapt forward to forty miles per hour and tucked in behind a green and red Eddie Stobart Lorry. 'Was the driver wearing a tie?' He wondered.

A discussion about global warming emerged self consciously from his radio. It sort of crept meekly out of the speakers because the human speakers themselves would leave whatever studio and climb into their Volkswagen blue polo and carry on polluting. Yes it would be a smidgeon less than a non blue polo but only a smidgeon he thought. And anyway the speaker had to get home quickly because he didn't want to miss his daughter's birthday treat at McDonalds. So he did drive at seventy five along the motorway.

Reg flicked back to Radio Two. The sport had finished. The Beach Boys were half way through 'Good Vibrations'. Should he overtake going up the Callow. No he couldn't be bothered. The lorry was doing fifty anyway. Plenty fast enough!

He turned into his drive. Rosamund was home before him. Her blue beetle abandoned with the boot lid not properly shut. Reg sat in his car listening to Roy Orbison finishing 'Pretty Woman'. 'Rosamund had never been pretty', he thought. But she was kind, easy to be with and live with; a wonderful 'Wife', she ironed his shirts and cooked a good roast. What more could a man ask for? Beautiful women were high maintenance and trouble. Besides which he wasn't exactly Charlton Heston himself. No, they made a good couple.

He leant over into the back and grabbed his briefcase. Forcing open the driver's door against the slight incline he clambered out and let gravity close the door.

"Is that you dear?" Rosamund, wearing long yellow primrose rubber gloves, was standing at the sink peeling potatoes.

"No." Replied Reg in a deep voice. "It's a sex crazed killer who's escaped from Wales with the sole intention of defiling and murdering English women who wear rubber gloves."

"Oh that's nice! Stick the kettle on love. Let's have a cuppa."

Reg put down his briefcase next to the telephone table in the hall. Took off his car coat and hung it on a stout wooden hanger in the hall cupboard, went through into the brightly lit kitchen, checked the water level in the kettle and flicked it on.

"You making or am I?" Reg inquired.
"Can you love? I'll finish the dinner."

Reg reached into the cupboard for two PG Tips pyramid tea bags. The kettle clicked off as he entered the left hand cupboard for two white IKEA mugs.

"Shall I take yours through, or do you want it here?" Triggered by his phraseology, a vision of Rosamund jumping backwards onto the work surface hoisting up her pencil slim grey skirt to reveal no knickers purring 'I want it here and now and I want it hard,' flashed through his mind.

"In the lounge if you don't mind love. The news'll be on the telly in a moment."

Reg took the two mugs through and put Rosamund's on a magazine resting on the arm of the settee. He set down his mug on the carpet in front of the other arm. Before he settled down he went back into the hall to get his newspaper from his briefcase. Seeing his lunch box he took it out, walked over and placed it on the draining board beside the dishwasher.

"Was your lunch OK dear?" Rosamund asked.

"No it was rubbish. I fed the sandwiches to the swans in the lake in Hyde Park when I flew down on a secret SAS training exercise to vet the company that makes and supplies Prince Williams condom's. There was a secret plot to blow off his dick and thus bring about the fall of the house of Windsor."

"Cheese and pickle tomorrow. I got the cheese you like from the Post office."
"Can you make sure it's Branston? The others are just cheap imitations."

Rosamund peeled off her gloves with an elastic 'thwack' Reg purposely stopped dead any lewd connotations with the noise by walking back into the lounge and switching on the TV.

"What's for dinner?" Reg inquired from the right hand corner of the long blue settee.

"Lemon sole, mashed potato peas and parsley sauce."
"Anything for after?"

"Yoghurt."

"Hope it's not that horrible fat free jelly muck?"

"No Waitrose Greek style honey yoghurt guaranteed to clog up your arteries in two spoonfuls."

"My life assurance is in the bottom drawer under my hated unused shirts."

"You only hate them 'cause you can't fit into them!" Rosamund smirked.

"Have a good day at work love?" Rosamund asked on autopilot as she viewed the evening BBC News.

"I bought some flowers. Cost me the best part of a tenner."

"Who for?"

"Me!"

Rosamund looked over towards her husband of thirty two years but he was engrossed behind the Guardian.

The phone rang in the hall.

"You or me?" Reg muttered. Rosamund didn't bother to answer. She got up, walked to the hall and answered.

Within ten seconds she was back with the handset.

"It's Pete for you." Reg took the handset.

"Pete, how goes it? What you up to?"

"Oh so so, you know how it is. Still living with the bitch from hell but too lazy and cowardly to do anything about it. Other than that, no money and I've got a cold."

"Pretty good then." Reg replied.

"Yes OK! Listen, what are you doing Saturday afternoon?"

"Let me check my diary. Ummmm! Private jet. Two p.m. Bristol airport with Richard (Branson) to Montecarlo to watch the GP followed by a private party on a yacht with the winner. Probably Schumacher. Yes, I know he's German but there are some things you just have to put up with."

"You're free then?"

"Yes!"

"Good, will you give me a hand? My aunt's recently died over at Worcester. She was eighty eight God Bless her, so she's had a good innings. Anyway, we've got to clear the house. My brothers hired a van to clear the furniture next Monday but he wants me to go and clear all the personal stuff, clothes, knick knacks, pictures, that sort of thing. He couldn't do it as they were pretty close. Do you fancy giving me a hand?"

"What time?"

"How about I pick you up at two?"

"That's fine. How much you going to pay me? My hourly rate is currently five hundred pounds an hour plus VAT."

"Two pints of Marston's Pedigree."

"Done. It's a deal; see you at two on Saturday."

"Pete OK?" Rosamund inquired, engrossed in the news.

"No he's dead."

"Don't be ridiculous, you've just spoken to him."
"I said. No, his aunt's dead. You're going deaf!"

Rosamund scowled at him and turned the volume down a notch to spite him. She knew he would struggle to hear and that he would say nothing.

"In the dining room or on your lap love?" Rosamund was blissfully unaware of the scenarios racing around his mind.
"Let's eat here. It's too cold in the dining room."

The lemon sole had been perfect. Reg cleared away the dishes into the kitchen simply so that he could raid the fridge and have some secret spoonfuls of honey yoghurt. So thick, creamy and delicious. He fluctuated between whatever TV programme she was watching, the Guardian and dozy sleep interrupted only by a cup of tea or a visit to the toilet.

The weather at the end of the ten thirty news signaled bedtime. Rosamund always cleaned her teeth religiously before bed. Reg knew he should but couldn't be bothered. Once a day was enough. He would wear his boxers; she always wore pyjamas or a nightie. At the moment she was on the left he was on the right but that was only because she could get a better view of the wall mounted TV. The age of passion and tenderness had long since passed. Now it was comfort and convenience. Reg always fell asleep before her.

"What you doing with Pete on Saturday?"
"Don't tell me you missed some of my telephone conversation?"
"Yes there was a good bit on the telly."
"Going to help clear out his aunt's house in Worcester?"
"Is that the one that's dead?"
"No! She's still alive. We're just stealing all her stuff to sell before we jet off to Las Vegas and put all the dosh on red. Of course she's dead!"
"Oh!---------Goodnight." Rosamund turned and disappeared into her own mind.
Turning quickly back she inquired "What time?"
"Two, why?"
"Thought I might go down to Sarah's and visit the kids. If you're out I'll have tea down there."
"OK I'll probably have something to eat in a pub with Pete."

Rosamund flicked off the TV with the remote. The room went dark.

Chapter 2.

Reg was standing at the front window watching the rain drops collide with the glass, trickle into each other and form downward rivulets that distorted the view. He wondered if the trickling drops had any capacity to change or affect the world. Today he was wearing dark blue corduroy trousers, concealing purple and black boxer shorts; black socks separated his feet from dark blue and white pumps. No vest, just a cream checked shirt and a thick comfortable beige cardigan with large dark brown leather covered buttons.

The white hire van pulled up at the bottom of the drive. Pete didn't get out. He sat there occasionally tooting until he saw a response. Slinging his coat over his head Reg pulled the front door shut and headed down the wet drive. Weeds were starting to grow again at the edge of the drive. It looked a mess. He decided tomorrow he would de-weed the drive and wiz over the lawn with the mower. It didn't really need it but it looked so much better when it was cut.
Quickly clambering into the passenger's seat he folded his damp coat onto his lap and buckled up.

"Go! Go! Go!"
"You been watching your boxed set of 'The Sweeney' then Reg?" Pete exclaimed.
"Yeh! Been thinking of chopping in the old Civic for a Three Litre Consul GT!"
"Reg I hate to tell you this but they stopped making them twenty five years ago."
"Well I never! Nobody told me that!" Pete turned the van in the narrow road and pointed it in the direction of the M50.

The house was atypical council. Semi-detached, concrete steps led down to a dark red front door with a brass Yale lock that at some time in its life had been brightly polished. The paintwork around it, ingrained with white dry polish. Now it was mottled with corrosive dried staining rain. The letterbox, the same, once cared for, but now neglected brass. The side of the house blocked off with a wooden garage. The unpainted wooden doors shut but not locked led to an empty space. The old gold Rover long gone after Syd had died.

"What was her name?" Reg asked.
"Edith but we kids always called her Aunty Edie. Aunty Edie and Uncle Syd. He worked at the sauce factory all his life, she was just a happy housewife and contented mother, no ambition just a happy family. This happiness thing's got to do with expectations Reg. Nowadays you're a failure unless you've got a ten inch dick, have sex at least once a day with your beautiful, slightly younger, slightly shorter wife with perfect thirty six inch tits, are rich, holiday abroad, work in IT and have a thrusting BMW. Cooking the Sunday roast for the family has gone out of the window as it were, along with women's bras. The old respectable society that lived in these houses has gone. Now it's low life and druggies who'd rather do anything than work. Even as low as stuffing themselves with chemicals and claiming it's not their fault. 'Sorry I'm a drug addict, I can't do any work but will you give me some of your money?' They really piss me off. This country's just too liberal. It'll all end in tears, you mark my words."
"What if there is no work Pete?"

"Rubbish. There's always work. Look at the Poles grafting in our fields in all weathers. Look at those Estonians washing cars by hand at the side of the road. Our lot are just too fucking idle to do the work. You've got to hand it to those commies they will at least get off their arses"

The door led into a small hall. The stairs started only a yard into the hall, the banister rail now yellowing fading cream. The cream and gold embossed wallpaper now starting to lift and curl as it yielded to cold and damp. A thin wood paneled painted door on the right led into the lounge. It was a trip back to the nineteen fifties. The wood veneered television had buttons to change the four channels. The mahogany HMV stereogram stood in the corner. Never used, except as a table. The flex had a round pin plug. The house had square pin sockets. Reg looked through the long playing records leaning in a slot. The Best of Perry Como, Kathleen Ferrier, Alma Cogan, Bing Crosby, Englebert Humperdinck. Frankie Vaughan. Lena Horne.

"What have we got to collect?" Reg nonchalantly asked.
"Everything that's not furniture or big." Pete yelled through from the kitchen.
"Have you got anything to put things in?"
"Yep! There's some heavy duty cardboard boxes in the back of the van. Can you get them in while I start sorting stuff?" Pete asked.
"It's like ripping the life out of a home." Reg commented to Pete. "What you going to do with it?"
"Keep what's good or anything I like, then sell the rest at a car boot."

"Will you check the loft Reg.? I've pulled my back a bit, lifting the last box. It should be empty. As far as I know they never used it. There's a pull down ladder and a light on your right."
"OK."

Reg clumped up the small stairs and went into the bathroom. The loo hadn't been flushed for months. He finished and flushed it but he couldn't hear it refilling.

Standing on a chair he removed the wooden hatch and eased down the hinged ladder. It was dusty. Clambering up each creaking aluminium rung he felt for the light switch and flicked it on. The loft lit up. A sea of orange fiberglass insulation floated between the joists. A pine timber walkway led to the water tank and the central heating tank. He looked around and saw nothing. Easing himself down the ladder he stopped to turn off the switch. He noticed that the insulation to the right of the tank rose about six inches higher. He could only see it because his eyes were at that level. Curious, Reg clambered into the loft and carefully navigated the thin creaking planks. Pulling aside the insulation revealed a dark burr walnut wooden box, dusty and festooned in orange fibres. An old simple key sprouted out of the single central lock. He lifted the box. It was heavy. He shook it and something thudded about inside. Placing it on the pine planks he turned the key to the left and unlocked it. Lifting the lid revealed an aged thick cardboard box bearing a picture of a revolver and the insignia of Smith and Wesson. Squashed in the corner was another plain square cardboard box. With trepidation he lifted the lid of the large faded blue box. A parchment stiff oiled rag lay on top. The rag was stiff to touch; the oil had dried and congealed making the cloth almost wax like. 'How many years?' Reg thought.
He lifted and removed the cloth. There it lay. Deep blue black metal, smooth as silk, hard as rock. Harder than rock! The checkering on the wooden grips sharp and unworn. No rust. Not a

blemish. Like new but old. Reg went to pick it up out of the box but stopped. What about the sweat and dirt on his hands? Would it rot away in a second if he touched it? A rude destructive awakening from its years of safe hibernation. He wiped his hands on his trousers, reached and picked it up. Such weight, such power, such beauty, such craftsmanship. A tag attached with string to the trigger guard revealed its owner. The ink fading but readable read 'Capt. James Alexander'. No date. Nothing more. Reg moved it about. It felt so comfortable, so good! An extension of his arm that gave him the power of life or death. He felt like a god. He had never felt that way before. He wrapped his forefinger around the smooth receptive trigger and watched the hammer begin its journey backwards. Sensibility kicked in. What if it were loaded? He hadn't checked. He eased the trigger back and the hammer dutifully followed. He could see four of the six chambers were empty. Looking carefully he found a button under the barrel. It moved easily and efficiently causing the chamber to spill open. The gun was empty. Reg inspected the mechanisms, the fluteing, the design. It had all been done with such care. Such precision. Such – dare he say it – love. It was a thing of almost artistic perfection. The symmetry, the balance. The power!

The sound of Pete moving about downstairs ripped him back into reality. Quickly he put it back into its cradle of shaped cardboard, replaced the rag and the lid. A shake of the small box confirmed what he suspected. Ammunition. The side of the box printed "50 Rounds Round Head .375 Calibre. The small box was heavy. Reg assumed it was full but he didn't open it and check.

"You coming Reg?" Pete shouted up from the lounge.
"Yep, be down in a sec." What to do now? He wanted to keep it. It fascinated him. Should he up front it with Pete and ask to have it? No Pete was a Policeman. A dear friend but a Police Officer nevertheless. It would be unfair to ask him to choose between right, wrong and Reg. He was in the loft of a Worcester council house having to make a choice which could give him immense satisfaction. He would cherish the gun. His secret. His darkness. His excitement. If he messed up he would certainly lose his friend, possibly his job, certainly his pension and maybe his liberty. If that happened he suspected he would lose his family as well.

Reg pulled open the box of ammunition. Fifty rounds pointed and glinted at him. Quickly he emptied the rounds into his hands and shoved some in his right trouser pocket. Some in his left trouser pocket. Some in his right trouser back pocket and the remainder in the left back pocket. The Gun. Where would be best to conceal it? He shoved it in his belt on his back. It felt acutely uncomfortable lodged between his trouser waistband and his kidneys. No, that would be really uncomfortable on the way back. Reg transferred it to the front. Wedging it down in front of his right groin. He felt like Butch Cassidy. The fat on his expanding girth cushioned the weapon. He buttoned up the two bottom buttons of the chunky loose knit cardigan concealing the wooden pistol grip from view

Reg turned the empty cardboard boxes upside down and locked the wooden box with the key leaving it in the lock

Clambering carefully down the ladder and flicking off the light he spoke to Pete.

"I found this old box in the loft Pete, There's nothing in it, just a couple of cardboard boxes." Reg purposely held and shook the box with one hand to indicate its emptiness.

"It's a lovely bit of Burr walnut though. I'd like to have it cleaned up and give it to Rosamund as a birthday present. It's her birthday in a fortnight and I know she'd really appreciate something like this to put her jewelry in."

Pete never gave the box a second glance.

"Sure Reg. Take whatever you want. It's really good of you to help me. Next stop 'The Travelers', yes? I could murder steak, chips, peas, mushrooms tomatoes and a couple of pints of bitter how about you?"

"Sounds good to me." Reg responded, trying to hide the absolute fear in his voice. 'What if the gun dropped out in the van, or in the car park, or in the Travelers Rest as they were walking in or out? What if Pete noticed the bulges in his pockets? It was very old ammunition. Would his body heat make it go off? The thought of bullets blasting his dick off in public flashed through his mind. You're Reg Moorcroft. Respected crime's analyst. What the fuck are you doing!' Reg pulled his coat over his uncomfortable lap and struggled with the seat belt as Pete drove away.

The grey wet evening quickly changed into a dark wet night. The wipers swishing continuously at the precipitous rain. The sound of the tyres changed with the different levels of water they cut through. Pete concentrated on getting them safely to the Travelers Rest Inn at the end of the M50 motorway. Conversation was limited by the noise.

The car park was half empty. Reg eased himself gingerly out of the van Leaving the box on the seat. He quickly got into his coat. The loose fit a godsend in covering up his secret. They hurried through the rain into the soft warmth of the restaurant come pub. Pints of dark brown Marston's Pedigree in hand they meandered over to an empty table near a window.

It was too hot to sit in his coat. It would be odd to do so. Reg stood up and took off his coat. The weight of the bullets was pulling his trousers down. He couldn't hitch them up. The gun might fall out. Folding his coat on the seat beside him he sat down and took a deep swig of his beer. He knew that the beer would soon relax him. Two pints would normally be enough to make the conversation light, humourous and truthful. He had to be on his guard. The steak was badly cooked and tough but neither himself nor Pete could be bothered with the hassle of a complaint. Reg could see Pete looked tired.

"Come on Pete. Drop me off home and get yourself off to bed. You look knackered."

"I am. Had to get up at five this morning for a job. Tomorrow I've got an early start taking Jessie and the kids to Alton Towers. That's not going to be a cheap day either. I tell you Reg I do loads of overtime but no matter how much money I make it's never enough. Jessie spends money like water, clothes, shoes, make up, hair and if I'm really honest I can't be bothered with the conflict of constantly challenging her about it. I just shut up and pay up. It's the weak man's quiet way out." The beer had turned on Pete's truthful tap.

"Wives and partners are pure luck Pete. Whether you get a good one or a bad one is pure luck. Sex, looks and kudos have a part to play at the start, but we never value prudence, thrift or pragmatism at the start. We never say "WOW look at her clothes, they're old but carefully looked after, do we? We never say 'she's so careful with electricity' do we? No! We say 'lovely tits' or 'great arse'. I tell you it's just luck. I got lucky with Rosamund."

Reg's house was in darkness as Pete dropped him off at the bottom of his drive. Rosamund wasn't home.

"Thanks for the help Reg. I do appreciate it." Pete spoke as Reg leaned back into the van to scoop up his box.
"Think nothing of it. That's what friends are for." Reg closed the door and headed up his drive. The bullets swayed and strained in his pockets. The box protected from the rain under his coat. The gun! The gun was stuffed in his waistband. Tight and pressing. An incompressible entity that demanded attention by its presence.

Reg unlocked the front door. As he entered he flicked on the lights. Sophia the cat rubbed and purred against his legs, following him quickly with tail erect into the kitchen hoping for some meat and milk.

He opened the wooden box and removed the two cardboard boxes. He felt in his pocket for the bullets. No, it was too dangerous. Rosamund may come home at any time. He couldn't risk it.

Picking up the wooden box he unlocked the back door and walked to his garden shed, come workshop, come sanctuary. The fluorescent tube flicked and blinked light into the large shed. Reg emptied out the fifty rounds of ammunition onto his workbench. Some of the lead bullets were showing signs of being polished as they had moved against the fabric of his pocket. They glinted and shone in a muted fashion. Reg packed them carefully into the cardboard box, some pointing upwards some nestling downwards in a perfect symmetrical fit.

Ammunition put to one side Reg reached into his cardigan and his belt. He felt the pistol grip slide so so easily into the palm of his hand. He slowly pulled it out. Even in the harsh white bright glare of the artificial light it looked perfect. Polished, honed, exquisite in its deadly form. Such control, such power. He couldn't get away from that word. It felt so powerful. He pulled the trigger and watched as his action rotated the chamber. The hammer flew forward with a hard unforgiving click as he caressed the trigger. Reg was surprised at how little effort it took to make it work. He pulled the hammer back by hand until it clicked and settled into the cocked position. A tiny pressure on the trigger released the hammer to fly forward.

Reg wiped it with the waxy stiff cloth and put it carefully back in its cardboard box. In the corner was a tub of old clothes Reg kept for rags. He positioned the two boxes half way down making sure they were well covered up.

He left the wooden box in clear view on top of the workbench. Turned off the light, locked up the shed and returned back to the kitchen to feed the cat.

Rosamund was in the kitchen. Engrossed in his thoughts and inner world he had neither heard nor noticed her return home.

"What you doing out in the shed?" She asked.

"Mind your own business. It's a secret. I'm allowed some secrets aren't I?"

"No." She pecked him on the cheek and gave him a cup of hot strong tea.

"OK! OK! You've caught me out. I've got a new woman in there."

"Who?"

"Nicole Kidman."

"Where's she going to sleep?"

"I've bought a camp bed from the Army and Navy."

"What about food?"

"She only eats one lettuce leaf a day."

"What about going to the toilet?"

"She doesn't go."

"Well that's very convenient for you dear. Do you want any tea or have you eaten?"

"Had half a tough old cow with Pete in the Travelers so a cup of tea will do nicely. How's the kids?"

"Margaret had croup last week. Sarah and Eric took her to the hospital, but she's OK now."

"Have they had any interest in selling the house yet? They'll have to move soon. The girls are growing up fast and that house is far too small plus it's only got that tiny backyard garden."

"I know but they seem happy enough and it's such hard work moving."

"Did you set the box to record X-factor?"

"Yes. I've told you before Reg, it records the whole series." Rosamund cast a resigned look at her husband sitting on the end of the long blue settee. Mug of hot tea in one hand trying to decide whether it was the TV or the newspaper that warranted his attention.

Chapter 3.

"Where's my tracksuit?" Rosamund looked at Reg in amazement.

"Probably buried under about ten years worth of old clothes in the back of the airing cupboard. Thinking of doing the marathon dear?"

"No, my job is sedentary. I'm sedentary, even the cat is sedentary. I need to get more physical exercise into my life before I die of sedentarism."

"There's no such word."

"There is, but if there isn't there should be. I thought I might take the car each morning and park on the top of the Doward and do a bit of speed walking around that track we used to walk 'round."

"Speed walking! That funny thing where your bottom jolts from side to side?"

"Yes I read an article. It's supposed to be very good for the heart and doesn't damage your joints. We have to be careful at our age."

"I'll get it out and give it a wash. When do you intend to start this regime?"

"Five o'clock tomorrow morning."

"Don't wake me up getting out of bed and don't flush the toilet."

"Why don't you come with me? We're both putting on a few pounds."

"No thanks, I need my beauty sleep. My skin needs time to rehydrate!"

Reg moved quietly as he could down the stairs. His once loose and voluminous tracksuit was now less loose, but it did smell fresh. He grabbed a small towel from the banister rail and curled it round his neck. A swig of semi-skimmed milk from the fridge freshened his mouth. He unlocked the back door as quietly as possible and made for the shed pursued by Sophia who bounced noisily through the cat flap.

Every time he touched, looked or handled the gun it excited him. This time more so. The six cartridges clinked and slid easily into the open chambers. Reg flicked the chamber shut with a flourish of his wrist. He'd seen it done in the movies but with the additional weight of the bullets it clunked satisfyingly shut. He positioned the gun in his waistband under his top but the moment he moved it started to slide down his leg. Shit he didn't want to have to carry it to the car just in case Rosamund peeped out of the window to wave him off. Looking round, he found an old bungee strop. It was short and only just stretched around his waist. It did the job. The gun was safely jammed against his stomach. The ends of the wire clips hurt a bit but it was tolerable for a short while. Pulling down the dark blue tracksuit top over the trousers concealed everything. He walked round the side of the house and into his car.

Although it was a light summer morning he had to use his lights. The dense full foliage of summer overhung from both sides of the steep narrow lane cut out most of the light. The Civic clawed its way up, emerging at the top into the green bright light of the just dawned day.

Reg locked the door and did a few warm up stretches. It was a long time since he'd done anything physical. He set off at a brisk space down the stony road. The gun digging into him. He was alone in the woods. Down and down he went into the old disused quarry.

Rabbits stared at the early morning human before hopping off to safety into a bramble clump. Woodpeckers savagely rattled away in short staccato bursts. A peregrine flew from perch to perch in front of him, annoyed by his intrusion.

Reg's heart was thumping but not from physical excursion. At the bottom of the quarry was an old derelict brick built shack. The stripped of paint wooden door hung on one hinge whilst nettles and thorns grew 'round its base. All the glass in the metal frames had long gone. Inside was just a concrete floor and a few discarded beer cans.

Reg had never fired a gun before. He didn't know what it felt like. He didn't know what it sounded like. He didn't know what it smelt like or what the bullet would do.

He had thought it through. He would fire off the six rounds quickly into the door and then climb quickly out of the quarry and resume his intended speed walk. If he met anyone who commented on hearing shots he would agree and suggest it was deer poachers.

The target was the door handle. He would try both ways, just pulling the trigger and cocking the hammer by hand.

He pulled out the gun from his stomach. It glinted and shone in the morning sun. He wondered when it had last been fired. Perhaps it had never been fired, he had inspected the bore and it looked perfect.

One hand or two. He decided two. Reg lined up the V sight and the notch on the end of the barrel with the door knob and slowly pulled the trigger. The hammer eased back then BANG! The huge explosion bounced and cracked around the wall of the quarry. Smoke wisped out of the end of the barrel. The door had a large smashed and splintered hole in it to the left of the doorknob. Jesus it was scary!! The recoil was strong as the barrel whipped upwards. Its job done and its energy spent.

Two more rounds thudded their way through the old timbers. The smell of cordite drifted off the gun. The oil began to seep with heat. Reg cocked the hammer by hand and took careful aim BANG! The old Bakelite door knob just disappeared. He re-cocked the hammer and turned to aim at an old fire some hundred yards away. The fire had the remnants of burnt food containers and beer cans. BANG! The explosion ricotched around the rock walls, the old fire remained intact. His final bullet hit an old burnt log some fifty yards away causing it to move back about a yard. The barrel of the gun now felt hot as he concealed it within his clothes and headed up the track and away from the quarry. God it was exciting! The smell, the sheer power, energy and destruction in the bullet. The sense of hidden secret capability. I can end someone's life if I want to. Not if I need to. Not if I must. Not if I have to, but if I want to! Reg felt so exhilarated he didn't notice the steep incline out of the quarry.

Reg hid the gun under the driver's seat and speed walked around the woodland track. It took him thirty two minutes. He noticed nothing of the absolute still summer beauty that surrounded him. He saw no one. A troop of about a dozen deer skipped over the track and disappeared into the woods. Their white hinds bobbing up and down as they skipped between the briars two hundred yards in front of him. His ears still rang and whistled with the blasts. 'How would it feel to be on the wrong end of such a weapon he thought? To have it pointed at you?' Now he really knew how powerful it was, the thought was at least calculable. Forty four bullets left! The sensation was intoxicating and addictive. He wanted more.

Reg was seriously puffing and panting by the time he had made it up the long incline back towards his car. The last quarter of a mile, more walk than speed, as the gradient increased. He unlocked the silver car twenty yards before he got to it. The flashing indicators welcomed him home. He wasn't as fit as he used to be, still, if he could stick to doing this most mornings he would soon lose a few pounds. He stopped to relieve himself by a bush. Very difficult in a tracksuit he had to pull down the strong elasticated waistband then sort of rested his dick on top of it. He watched the flow as it built up in a small puddle on the ground then start to trickle downhill. He wondered if it was a Tsunami in a bacterial or insect world. Had he killed something by having a piss?

He opened the door and was immediately hit by the strong smell of burnt cordite. Collapsing into the driver's seat he wiped his face and neck with the small towel then had a good spit. Closing the door he turned on the ignition and dropped all four electric windows. The Radio burst into life with Sarah Kennedy doing her "bored, tired of this" early morning show. Still at least she was there and not ill, on holiday or just failed to turn up. The cold early air was welcome as he cruised down the hill to home.

"Is that you love?" Rosamund called out from upstairs as she heard the front door open.
"No it's a Neanderthal humanoid life form that's just escaped from a cave deep in the Doward hill, hell bent on rape and pillage."
"Be a love and feed the cat."

Rosamund pecked him safely on the cheek as she fled, late, out of the front door.
 From the front door of her car she shouted "Your lunch box is in the fridge. There's a bit of cake in it, left over from the weekend. Lemon drizzle. Your favourite."
"Oh, OK, thanks." Reg replied as the diesel engine of her beetle throbbed into life.

He watched her drive off then went into his car. The gun, carefully wrapped in rags, was still warm. The now empty brass cartridge cases rattled in their chambers. Moving quickly around the side of the house he made the shed. He must clean it. He'd read that the cordite was highly corrosive and the barrel must be cleaned after use. He hadn't time to do it properly and reached for his new can of WD40. A strong spray of the fluid down the barrel and into the chambers should do the trick. The smell of WD 40 mingled with that of the cordite. It was quite pleasant. He liked it. Sort of masculine and efficient. Wiping the gun nearly dry he returned it to the box hidden in his bag of rags.

Allan Mayor knocked on Reg's office door and came in.

"Got any info on these Subaru ram raiders Reg? Truckers Garage got done last night on the A40. The car was a white Sierra Cosworth 4x4 but we kind of think it was the same gang. Fast car, four seats and four wheel drive. No plates on it obviously. CCTV shows just four well covered males wearing balaclavas can't even tell black or white."

"Not at the moment Allan but I'm going to Birmingham tomorrow for a conference with West Mids about ram raiders so come and see me on Wednesday. I hear you're getting married."
"Bad news travels fast, as they say." Allan laughed.
"How old are you Allan?" Reg asked.
Allan looked at him reproachfully. "Twenty three. Why?"
"First real girlfriend? First time you've been in love?"
"As it happens, yes."
"Good luck! Oh Allan, before you go can I ask you to do something illegal and highly dangerous for me?"
Allan was now looking totally bemused and puzzled. "What?"
"Can you get me about a dozen of those thick white cable ties they use as emergency handcuffs from the charge room? I've got some young trees in my back garden and they keep bending over in the wind,"
"See what I can do." Allan winked as he closed the office door.
Reg turned back to his computer. Better check exactly what we have got on ram raiders before my trip tomorrow. He thought.

"Might be late tomorrow night. Going to Birmingham for a conflab about these bloody ram raiders. I'll get a McDonalds on the way home."
"I'll just have salad and pasta then." Rosamund replied from her end of the settee.

"Got anything for me Reg?" Allan knocked and entered at the same time bearing a brown thick paper property bag with concealed content.
"Sit down Allan. It looks like a gang of four Afro-Caribbean lads from Digbeth. All of the stolen four by fours are from Digbeth or the surrounding areas. No plates recorded at the scenes of course but their M.O. is to torch the vehicle after they've finished with it. DS Parkinson from West Mids is the guy to talk to but there will be a pack coming out soon. The priority at the moment is to identify vulnerable premises and strongly advise them to spend some money on bollards."
"Okey Dokey Reg I'll get that organized. Thanks very much. Here's your stolen goods. For gods sake don't tell the police." He winked as he was leaving.

Reg took one of the cable ties out and inspected it. Just a patent number.

"Happy birthday to you! Mashed potatoes and stew! Bread and butter in the gutter! Happy birthday to you!" Reg burst into their bedroom in just his underpants carrying her carefully wrapped present and a card. Leaning over he kissed her tenderly on the nose.

"Wake up! It's your birthday!"

Rosamund sat up and rubbed her eyes then looked at him and the present.

"What is it?"

"How the bloody hell should I know? It was delivered by some sharp dark young Latino in a blood red Ferrari F40. He wanted to sing underneath your bedroom window but I told him to sod off as I couldn't understand Italian."

Rosamund carefully removed the thick, expensive paper. The polished old walnut looked deep and beautiful in the morning sun. The small central lock and key now polished and cleaned to reveal its true brass colour, matched by the full length brass hinge at the back. The box looked good from any and all angles. She turned the key and eased open the lid. The inside, now compartmentalized and clad in new deep green baize.

"It's beautiful Reg. I wondered what you were doing nipping back and forth to the shed all the time."

"Thought you could put all your diamonds and jewelry in it. You know! Makes it easy for a burglar to steal if it's all in one place." She kicked out at him from underneath the duvet then put her arms around him and kissed his neck.

"Thank you. You old romantic."

"I'll have less of the old if you don't mind. I suppose you'll be wanting a cup of tea in bed seeing as it's your birthday."

"Of course!" Rosamund inspected the box from all sides and stroked the highly polished wood. "It's lovely Reg. Where did you get it?"

"Stole it." Said Reg leaving the bedroom.

Reg woke with a jolt from a doze on his end of the settee.

"Who got booted off?" He asked Rosamund.

"Tracy."

"That's a shame. I liked Tracy."

"Well it's your fault you should have stayed awake and voted for her. Do you fancy a cuppa?"

"Oh yes please. Got to go to Birmingham again on Friday for another one of those Crime Conferences. I'm going to take my car to Ledbury and catch the train. I can't be doing with the hassle of parking. I might be late back depending if I have a drink or not. I'll see how I feel."

"That's OK I'm out on Friday night. Having a drink with Cynthia, find out all the gossip about her disgusting lover."

"Why's he disgusting? Is he depraved or something."

"He's disgusting because she's totally besotted with him and he treats her like shit."

"Perhaps she likes being treated like shit." Rosamund threw a quick 'are you totally mad' glance at him.

"Have you had a shave today?"

"No. I've got a really itchy rash under my chin. I thought I'd knock off shaving for a week, see if it'll settle down. I'll have one of those grey designer stubble beards. I expect people will start mistaking me for George Clooney and ask for my autograph when I go to a coffee machine."

The second 'are you totally mad' glance sliced its way towards him.

It was eight years ago that Reg hid it behind the immersion tank in the airing cupboard. Rosamund had gone shopping in Cheltenham. She would be hours. He pulled out old pillows, sheets, pillowcases and even some old clothes. Kneeling down he reached behind the tank. His fingers felt something soft and polythene, He grabbed it and pulled it out. Yes! There it was looking like a brown dead rat ensnared in a plastic bag.

He pulled out the wig and positioned it onto his bald plate. Jiggling it around he decided that if you were half blind in one eye and cataracts in the other it looked OK. All the kit was still there to fix it to his shiny head. He packed it all away and hid it under the spare bed in the back bedroom.

Reg eased and inched his car into the tight space in Morrison's car park. It was only eight in the morning but already some quasi uniformed retired robot was collecting car numbers in the half empty car park. The store had only just opened. Everything normal was now heightened and scary. He started to sweat with excitement as he entered the store. Not bothering with a pound released trolley, he opted for a basket and headed for the fruit counter. There they were. Just what he wanted. Big dark green striped rugby balls masquerading as watermelons. He picked the biggest and put it in his basket. What a weight! He scratched at his itchy beard and made for the electrical aisle. Morphy Richards travel electric razor. Thirty two pounds, special offer, that will do. He picked the box off the shelf and dropped it into his basket. Making for the tills he passed a display of Welsh Cakes. He loved Welsh Cakes. A pack jumped into his basket. He thought it highly ironic that here he was, about to do something staggeringly monumental and hunger was still a factor in his day.

The fat ugly made up young girl scanned his shopping. The omnipresent beeps her only motivation.

"Thirty four pounds fifty." No please or smile. "Do you want a bag?"
"Yes Please."
"Regular or 'for Life'?" Reg wondered how long, in his particular case 'for life' would be?
"Does the 'For Life' one have a zip?"
"Yes"
"For life please."
"That's another twenty pence then." At no time had she looked at him.

Reg picked up the receipt and the change from his two twenty pound notes from off the hard stainless steel down sloping loading shute.

"Have a nice day." She uttered without taking her eyes away from the electronic till.

Reg put his melon and razor in the green and red 'for life' bag and left.

Munching on his Welsh Cakes calmed him as he drove the twelve miles to Ledbury. He reached under his seat and put the bulky Waitrose carrier bag into his 'bag for life'.

Reg liked Ledbury station. It was a 1950's time capsule. There was always room in the car park. The parking was free and the man who sold you the tickets was polite, courteous and helpful. The tickets were dispensed from what was, in effect, a wooden shed, adorned with railway memorabilia. He liked sheds.

By now it was raining, not heavily but spasmodic. Reg rummaged in the Morrison's bag for the razor. He took it out of the box and flicked it on. It worked but only just. The battery was weak. Getting out of his car he put on his coat, black side out. Picked up the bag and discarded the razor box in a litter bin. The charger he stuffed into the pocket of his coat. The bag was quite heavy.

"Day return to Richmond please?"
"Now would that be Richmond Surrey or Richmond Yorkshire?" The ticket office man wearing his peaked cap inside the wooden office asked.
"Yorkshire."
He tapped into the machine and winced.
"Not cheap Sir."
"How much?"
"One hundred and eleven pounds eighty."
"Oh well. Needs must and all that." Reg was acting. Inside he thought the price was exorbitant, but this reaction paled into insignificance with what he was about to do.
"Platform two across the bridge next train to Birmingham, gets in at 11.13, or at least it's supposed to. 1130 connection to Darlington and then the 14.33 connection to Richmond. Gets in at 1504. What time you coming back?"
"Don't know yet. Depends what time my meeting finishes."
"Well, the latest you can leave is the 18.05 from Richmond, that should get you back here at 23.38 if all goes well."
"OK. Thanks."

Reg lugged his heavy bag over the bridge and waited along with two other men and a young woman with a pushchair for the two tone green train. Within five minutes it was there.

Business men with laptops were everywhere. He couldn't help wondering what was so important in their lives that required them to tap away at god knows what whilst commuting through Colwall Malvern Worcester Droitwich and Bromsgrove. He decided it was nothing. They were just playing the part. Dynamic, focused, dedicated, valued and seemingly important men. He plugged in the charger to his cheap shaver and connected it up. A little orange light told him it was charging. The young woman with the baby looked strangely at him. Had it been a mobile phone or an Apple Netbook she wouldn't have noticed but a shaver! Well that was different.

The route and scenery to Birmingham was familiar. He knew all the stops. He concentrated on looking out of the window. He couldn't allow himself to consider or think about what he was doing.

The route northwards out of Birmingham was unfamiliar. That made it easier. Watching the changing landscape as they rattled and surged northwards took his mind off things.

The grass changed colour. It was still green but somehow lighter and more sparse. Hedgerows started to change into limestone dry stone walls. Hills became a more prevalent part of the overall scenery. Rock became commonplace. By the time Sheffield and Leeds had passed his shaver was fully charged.

The change at Darlington gave him twenty minutes. He was hungry but couldn't eat. Thirsty but afraid to drink in case he needed the loo at an inconvenient moment. No! He waited on the platform for the grey two unit local train to arrive.

The train blasted its two tone noise and rattled out of the station south towards Richmond. The train was almost empty. He reached into his bag and pulled out the Waitrose carrier, stood up and headed for the toilet. Once inside he looked at himself long and hard in the mirror. He looked pale and nervous. Reaching into the bag he brought out the wig, he straightened it out and fixed it carefully into position. He looked at a changed man. The wig was OK if you didn't look too hard. At just a glance, it looked almost real. There was a colour difference, the remaining hair on the side of his head was now mottled with grey but it wasn't too bad. He reached back into the bag and brought out eight of the white wide cable ties. Reg carefully curled them into a pocket. He hoped that would be enough. His final delve into the bag brought out the gun. He looked at it. Its brutal weight and presence gave him confidence. Reg flicked open the chamber and spun it. Six brass cartridges glistened. The copper percussion caps in the center of each one, soft and protected. He clicked it shut and slid it butt down into his left inner pocket. It fitted well. He didn't want it to fall out.

Reg slid back the lock and went back to his seat. No one noticed that a bald man had gone into the toilet and a man with hair had come out.

The train was coming to a halt. The computerized message told him that 'This Is Richmond'. He waited by the door. Two young men with bikes were also waiting for the train to come to a halt.

"How far is it from the station to the Market Square?" Reg asked. The dark haired youth responded.
"It's really close; it takes about five minutes if you walk fast."
"Thanks." Said Reg.

The train stopped and he got off. By now his heart was audibly pounding. A five minute walk would do him good. It was cloudy and overcast but not actually raining although it had been judging by the wet gutters. Reg followed the signs to the centre of town. The watermelon was becoming increasingly heavier; he questioned his decision to bring it. Perhaps he wouldn't need it. What a waste of one pound fifty. He reached into his right hand pocket and put on a new pair of cream thin leather pilot's gloves. The leather was so thin and supple that they were almost unnoticeable.

There it was, directly in front of him. Two front windows displaying services and deals, above the windows in green lettering 'THE YORKSHIRE BUILDING SOCIETY'.

'For fucks sake turn around and go home Reg Moorcroft. What the fuck are you doing?' His whole life and world was screaming at him. 'Don't do it!'

Reg stood there looking at the pinkish tinged sandstone building. The watermelon in the Morrison's for life bag in his right hand. The gun rested and pulled on his left front. He turned away from the kerb and caught sight of himself in a shop window.

Unkempt windblown wig, scruffy almost beard in a black car coat. Mr. Nobody. If he died right there and then nobody would be affected with the exception of his immediate family. The world wouldn't know or care. He'd leave nothing behind of any lasting value. A few sad comments and life would go on.

He turned quickly to face the road and the building society office on the other side. Stepping out into the road totally focused he suddenly heard a screech of locked tyres coming from his right. A well worn transit van shuddered to an emergency stop inches from him.
A young Yorkshire male leaned out of the window and yelled at him.
"You need to get some glasses you stupid old bastard!"
Reg ignored the tirade and continued across the road. The door to the building society office was locked. There was a green button on the door jam next to the handle. Reg pressed it. A woman from behind the glass screened counter peered at him. He smiled.
She reached under the desk and the door buzzed. He pushed the door open and entered. There was only one customer. A grey haired man clearly in his seventies. A service desk with three glass screened points led over to a stout wooden access door protected by a push button security lock. The whole thing served to separate the front customer end from the rear staff end. He could see five females behind the desks. No males. Reg transferred his Morrison's bag into his left hand and reached in for the gun. It came out barrel first. His left hand and the bag came up to momentarily assist his right hand whilst he grasped the grip in his palm and got his finger on the trigger. In an instant there was a massive explosion and the glass screen shattered. The women screamed and threw themselves to the floor. The old man stood there mesmerized, transfixed and motionless. The second blast literally blew away the security lock on the door, slamming the door itself back on its hinges into the wall. The noise from the two shots was horrendous when confined in a small space. Much worse than the quarry. Reg waved the still smoking gun at the old man and indicated for him to move into the back. A few people looked in through the glass door window but quickly ran away when they saw the gun.

"If any one moves they will not get out of here alive." Reg spoke authoritatively.
He looked at the name tags they were wearing. Kathleen Thomas Manager. The gold lettering said on her badge.

"Stand up Kathleen Thomas." Reg commanded. She dutifully rose. Reg delved into his coat pocket and produced five cable ties. He gave them to her.

"Put your colleagues and that customers hands behind their backs and secure them tightly. Do not worry, I will check that you've done it properly."

"DO IT QUICKLY AND DO IT NOW!" Reg half cocked the hammer and pointed the gun at the old man. He was empowered. He wasn't the office Reg any more. He was strong, commanding. He was a different man.

Kathleen Thomas frantically did as she was told. Her nerves and shaking made it difficult to thread the ties.

"Now use your manager's keys and open up the strong room."
"I- I- I can't." She stammered. It's on a time lock released from head office."
"I don't believe you! It's business hours you would not have to contact head office every time you wanted a bit of money."
"It's true! It's true!" She pleaded.

Reg took her gently by the hand and led her to a chair by a table. He turned the chair with its back against the wall.

"Please sit down." She did as she was told. She was frightened witless. Reg put another chair on the other side of the table, again with its back against the wall. Moving quickly he assisted one of the tied up assistants onto the chair. He moved towards his bag and took out the melon. Placing it exactly between them on the table he stood two yards back and fired. It was as though the whole room had exploded. The sound and shock waves contained and deafening. The watermelon literally disintegrated showering the two cowering women in red wet pulp. Reg fired another round five seconds later to the left of the other woman's head. A huge chunk of masonry fell away as the heavy bullet embedded itself in the wall. The room began to fill with smoke and dust.

"Alright! Alright! I'll open it." Kathleen Thomas gasped.

She fumbled with the large bunch of keys retrieved from her handbag and unlocked the two locks. She finally punched in the code to the security timer then eased the door open.

It was a cream painted well lit strong room. Surprisingly empty. On the end shelves at the back were neat bundles of fifty, twenty and ten pound notes. Reg gave her the Morrison's bag.

"Fill it up. Fifties first then twenties and if there's any room left tens." She scurried in scooping the rubber band wrapped bundles into his bag. Reg remained at the door watching and waiting. Within thirty seconds she'd finished. The bag was full.

"Zip it up please and give it to me then bring your handbag and come with me."

Reg and his hostage moved towards the back door.

"Open it." He commanded. She fumbled and unlocked the door. They moved outside.

"Lock it then give me the keys and your car keys." Kathleen searched in her bag for her car keys.

"Which is your car?" He inquired.

"The silver Renault Clio over there."

"Do I need a pass to get through the car park barrier?"

She dove into her handbag again and quickly handed over the plastic bar coded card.

Reg led her discreetly back to the rear door of the building society and opened the door. He used a cable tie to secure her hands behind her back then gently pushed her inside and locked the door.

The Clio started first time. He drove calmly and slowly out through the barrier and into the town. He headed for Tesco's. Once mobile he slipped the gun back into his inside coat pocket. He drove into the crowded car park and found a spot in the middle of the busiest area, parked, left the keys in the ignition and walked away with his bag out of the car park and towards the station. He figured it would be at least late tonight before Tesco's rang in the vehicle and their CCTV would record the same bearded brown haired man.

It took him twenty minutes to walk to the station. He didn't hurry; he was an old man with a Morrison's 'for life' carrier bag. The spitting rain felt good. He could hear sirens heading towards the centre of town.

There was no ticket inspector at the station. Reg caught the 17.10 train for Darlington.

Ten minutes into the journey he went to the toilet with his bag. Locking the door he ripped off the wig and took off his coat. Reg reversed it so the tan colour was outside. Taking out his Waitrose bag he wrapped the gun in its rag then put it into the thin green and white plastic bag, folding it and knotting the handles as well as he could to prevent the cordite smell from escaping. He reached into his pocket, took out his shaver and switched it on. The rotating blades chewed their way painfully and slowly through his dense tough growth. Occasionally they clogged up and stopped altogether. It was a long uncomfortable process and now he really did have a bad rash under his chin but he no longer had a beard. The wig and the keys to the Richmond office of the Yorkshire Building Society were quietly dropped out of the window.

"Tickets please?" The scruffy young ticket inspector scribbled on his ticket and moved on. Reg jammed the bag between his feet and watched the summer evening clatter by.

Chapter 4.

"You're home late love. Did you have a good day?" Rosamund got up from the settee to make him a cup of tea.

"The usual, you know. Strained quiet start, blah blah blah, coffee and a few biscuits that you really want to dunk but daren't for fear of being labeled an uncouth moron. More blah blah blah, Lunch, usual picky buffet and orange juice. Blah blah blah, coffee, blah jokes blah jokes. Someone suggests a pint in the local, one stretches to three then we're hungry so time to track down the local curry house and here I am home late."

"Never mind, here's your tea. Don't fall asleep with it in your hand and spill it over your trousers again. I see what you mean about that rash, it hasn't gone has it? I'll get you some cream from Boots tomorrow."

"Rosamund --?"

"What?"

"Nothing, it's OK."

Rosamund turned back to watch Jeremy Paxman savage his current victim.

Reg drank his tea feeling uncomfortable. The gun was used and dirty in the plastic bag. He couldn't clean it 'til at least tomorrow morning. He imagined the corrosive cordite eating away at the almost pristine bore.

"You going speed walking tomorrow morning?" Rosamund asked.

"Yes if it's dry."

"We better get to bed then."

"Good weekend Reg? What did you do? Weather was rubbish as usual." Corrallee called out as Reg ambled passed her desk, tan coat on his right arm black briefcase in his left hand.

"Nothing much. Police escort and sirens up to Faslane Naval base, Atomic powered submarine, thirty five knots per hour under water all the way to the site of the Titanic then torpedo and sink a private submarine owned by a conglomeration of Irish and Libyan terrorists who were trying to refloat it with balloons and sell it on Ebay."

"Did you manage to paint your garage door then?"

"No but I got the undercoat on between the showers"

Allan Mayor was waiting outside Reg's office looking like a Cheshire cat on speed. Reg unlocked his office and entered with Allan close behind.

"We got them Reg. We got the bloody Ram Raiders." Allan was jubilant.

"How?" Reg asked, hanging up his coat and putting down his briefcase.

"Well it was down to you really. After our little chat I did what you said. I drew a list of all potentially vulnerable properties then got the lads to go round and warn the owners. Anyway one of the garage owners said he noticed two iffy looking black lads in a smart Subaru Impreza. They didn't have fuel, they just came in for one bag of crisps. He said their eyes were everywhere. We checked his CCTV tapes, got the number and low and behold it's a nicked vehicle from Solihull; put it out on PNC and on Saturday afternoon it's pulled in Redditch."

"Fantastic!" Reg responded.

"It gets better." Allan jigged about. "In the boot was some of the nicked gear from our Truckers job they must have been trying to punt it out." Allan shook Reg's hand vigorously.

"Thanks Reg. You're a star!" Allan left the office as though he was on cloud nine.

Reg looked at his right hand and considered.

There was nothing on his computer about Richmond in Yorkshire. He knew that in Yorkshire and its surrounds, algorithms would be crunching their way through trillions of ones and zeros looking for anything or anyone that matched the crime.

"I'll be away the weekend after next. Got to go to Scotland. To Edinburgh, there's a Crimes Analysis convention that the boss wants me to attend."

"Oh that's a pity Reg, it's little Neil's birthday party that Saturday he's two."

"Can't be helped, I've ducked out of most of the dross but this one I've got to attend."

"Never mind we'll get him something nice. I was thinking of a pedal car, what do you think?"

"Sounds good, I'll have a look on the internet, see if I can get him something traditional made of metal, not something that's come out of a plastic mould in China."

"Well don't go mad Reg, he's only two, we don't want an Aston Martin replica in the lounge."

"OK! OK! A Maserati then." Rosamund looked over with disdain towards her childish meek and mild husband.

Reg came out of Boots and turned right. It was warm and sunny; people were beginning to wear shorts. He crossed the road and made towards the bookshop on his left. He often wondered how it survived. He surmised that it must be a labour of love for the ageing gentle male owner. Opening the door and walking in made a bell tinkle. How quaint he thought. He wanted two books; it didn't matter what they were. The only criteria being their thickness. The thicker the better. He found them easily. One about medication the other about Zoology. They cost him twelve pounds. He paid cash and left with the heavy books in a plain white carrier bag.

Reg locked his office at 17.02 on Friday evening and made his way to the stairs.

Glennys was just putting on her coat.

"Jumping the gun a bit aren't you Reg? It's usually at least five past."

"Trying to re-adjust my work-life balance." Reg flung back as he briskly walked towards the office door.

"Come on! Come on! Come on!" Reg tapped impatiently on the steering wheel as the barrier wafted through vehicles one at a time. Turning right instead of left at the T junction he headed for Fownhope and Gloucestershire. On the back seat was a black Adidas sports bag. Rosamund had packed him three clean shirts (He only needed two but she figured he might spill something down one of them) clean socks and pants, a pair of black corduroy trousers, his razor, shaving foam, deodorant toothbrush and paste. He had no use for a comb. Reg had added the two thick books from out of the boot. In his pocket was five thousand pounds in fifty pound notes. In his wallet was three hundred pounds in tens and twenties. In his back pocket was his passport.

The rush hour traffic cleared after Fownhope village. Reg pressed on quickly in his normally sedate civic. It was six o'clock as he turned into the gates of Staverton airport. The Gloster Javelin gate sentry, a sad reminder of Britain's independent aviation past.
He parked and locked the car behind Helo-Ferry's offices and walked around the building to the hard standing. A shiny white helicopter was impatiently waiting for it's customer, it's rotors swishing and biting at the warm evening air.

"Mr. Moorcroft?" One of the ground crew asked.
Reg nodded.
"Your flight awaits you, here's your receipt in case you need it for expenses."
"I don't." Reg answered. The crewman escorted him in under the blades and strapped him in. The Helicopter clattered skywards.

"What time's your flight?" The co-pilot turned and asked.
"Eight fifteen."
"No problem, it takes about forty five minutes from here to Heathrow."
"How do I get from where we land to Terminal five?"
"How are you travelling, first, business or economy?"
"First."
"Not a problem, we'll radio ahead and a car will be waiting for you."

The black Toyota Lexus scooped him up and dropped him outside Terminal five. By seven fifteen he was checking in.

"Would you like to take dinner in the Concorde Lounge or onboard Sir?" The professionally charming hostess inquired.
"It'll be rushed if I eat before so I'll wait and eat onboard." Reg wasn't used to the service and consideration that money bought. He liked it. The machine produced his boarding pass.
"Boarding will commence at 19.45 Sir."

Reg made his way to the Concorde lounge. Really it was just an 'Officers Club' The only requirement for entry – Money. The large airy lounge, simply an opulent shed. The stressed white struts and girders, lit and displayed were there to keep the roof on and make the building stand up. Architectural laziness, he thought! Don't bother to conceal the ugly bits. Make a feature of them. He sat down in a large comfortable grey easy chair with a window view and watched civil aviation parade before him. A glass of champagne and a dish of olives helped him to relax. An immaculate young woman came over and discreetly told him that his aircraft was now boarding.

A good meal served on bone china with more champagne led to a comfortable horizontal sleep for the rest of the four hour journey. Midnight in Moscow actually meant three fifteen AM. Reg made his way to the near deserted VIP lounge and sank into an easy chair to await his nine forty hop to Nizhny Novgorod airport.

The Avia Air Embraer 120 turboprop aircraft was the exact opposite to British Airways first class. Small, noisy and cramped, it safely deposited thirty people at the provincial city airport of Nizhny Novogod at ten fifty five. With no hold luggage to collect he was one of the first to exit the airport. Amongst the waiting congregation was a chubby flaxen haired short Russian driver with a green peaked cap and a placard stating R. Moorcroft. Reg headed in her direction. Her English was stilted and awkward but together they smiled and gestured. The car, black and heavy with chrome, was comfortable and warm. The city, unremarkable and typically unpretentious, swept quickly by. Reg was in an alien world where nothing registered. Buildings, trees, bridges, fields, parks, churches, just seemed to merge into an unfathomable scenario. Then there they were, entering the first security post of Dolinsk Sokol Military Airbase. The historic home of Russian MIG jet fighters. Papers, permits, copies of visa and passport were passed out, inspected and returned. On the left was a row of historic MIG fighters. 15,s 19,s 21,s 25,s and finally a 29, its sharp aggressive profile in direct contrast to the more rounded 'friendlier' predecessors. Two more security posts were successfully passed before the big black car swept out into the airbase heading for a cluster of huts and hangers on the other side of the vast concrete and grass facility.

"Hi my name's Dimitri. You haven't paid yet. How do you want to pay?" Dimitri's voice was like him. Thick set and heavy. The fair hair and blue eyes sat on top of a strong jaw with just a hint of developing jowls.

"Cash, English Pounds."
"Deposit of two thousand pounds you paid by credit card. Do you have fifteen thousand pounds cash with you?"
"Yes." Reg produced a roll of a hundred fifty pound notes from his pocket and handed it over.
"There's five thousand." He unzipped his bag and pulled out the two old thick books. Dimitri looked bemused.
"There's five thousand in that one and five thousand in this one." Reg started extracting the flat individual notes from out between the pages.
Dimitri did as Reg.
"Fifteen thousand pounds cash English." Dimitri confirmed after fifteen minutes.
He held out his hand, this time smiling. "Welcome to Fulcrum Flights Mr. Moorcroft. How was your journey? Pleasant I hope?"
Reg reciprocated his change in attitude.
"It was OK Dimitri. Now, what do I do now?"
"Now we begin your trip of a lifetime. I promise you will never have a better experience than this. Follow me"

Reg followed in the wake of Dimitri who was still clutching his fifteen thousand pounds. A dark green timber door led into a room manned by a small young man. The paraphernalia was that of a medical nature. A blood pressure check and a questionnaire of 'have you ever suffered from' questions led to his signing of a disclaimer. Dimitri disappeared out of the room but reappeared a few minutes later minus the cash.

"Your flights at two thirty so we've got plenty of time to kit you up. I would advise you to skip lunch. Follow me we have a practice ejection seat. I will show you the drill."

The drill left Reg dangling from a harness in a Russian shed

The next shed saw him kitted out in an Anti-G suit, a flying overall, a life jacket and a helmet. It wasn't 'til he saw Dimitri climbing into the same gear that Reg realized Dimitri was his pilot.

Out from the final room and into the afternoon sun brought them face to face with the blue and white MIG 29 Military jet fighter. It's pod-like double cockpit arched out in front of the plane like something from a Star Trek movie. The twin rudder fins at the rear sprouted at angles that looked just right. The sloping back rectangular air ducts for the engines were slung underneath like two yawning coffins ready to gulp and use the air they breathed. The whole vicinity smelt of burnt paraffin. The afterburner shrouds still cracked and clicked as the metal cooled. Silver slender complicated oleo legs supported the hawkish craft. Pipes and leads tethered the machine down. It looked like a sleek skittish stallion that would prance away at the slightest chance. The cockpit was hinged open.

Dimitri led the way towards the plane. Reg followed as Dimitri made a close physical examination of the aircraft. Looking at, feeling and shaking the six stores carriers underneath the wings. The various tubes and sensors that emerged at odd places. The Tyres and removable panels underneath the fuselage. Eventually he was satisfied and ordered Reg up the ladder. Reg eased his way into the rear cockpit. The seat sprouted the red double D –Do not touch unless you're about to Die - handles from between his legs. A friendly ground crew man strapped him in, pointed out the rudder pedals and gesticulated which way the aircraft would turn if you pushed with your left or right. The joystick, throttle levers and some of the main instruments. Another technician was strapping in Dimitri. The large back hinged Perspex canopy remained open as Dimitri started up the engines. The gentle swoosh of their start up phase soon turned into a positive hot exhaust as the turbines built up speed deep underneath them.

The ground crewman removed some red tagged pins from the ejection seat and stowed them in a metal block on the left bulkhead. He mouthed "Good luck" as he climbed down the ladder and removed it. Reg was alone in his cockpit. Separated from Dimitri by a black riveted hump that housed instruments. He was surrounded by functional tough looking instruments, dials, switches, displays and buttons. The large blue/grey helmet felt heavy and cumbersome on his head. The intercom crackled into life.

"Please put on your oxygen mask Mr. Moorcroft." Reg clipped it up into position and spoke back.
"OK Dimitri, it's on." The straps holding Reg into the seat were very tight. He felt 'compressed'.

Dimitri and the crewman swapped waves, Chocks were pulled away from the wheels and the sharp angled blue and white fighter lurched forward only to jolt to a standstill as he tested the brakes. Released from the brakes it cruised forward, jet exhaust gently wafting and whistling from the two massive after burner tubes. Thin sharp anhedral wings itching to dig deep into soft Russian air.

The aircraft turned in its own length to line up with the runway. The cockpit lowered slowly then hissed as locks slid home and seals inflated. Reg's life was in the hands of a five foot eleven

Russian he had only met three hours ago. The runway with its black rubber marquetry undulated before them. He couldn't see the end. Dimitri was talking to the tower, first in Russian, then in English. Reg heard 'Fulcrum 002 you are clear for take off'

"Feeling OK Mr. Moorcroft?" Reg's intercom asked.
"Fine, Just fine Dimitri." It was not a lie. Reg Moorcroft was excited by his nervousness and relishing the unknown that lay before him.

There was no gentle acceleration. The throttles were pushed forward, the craft arched upwards for a second as the brakes held then!

The massive acceleration pushed him so hard back into his seat he felt that the belts were loose. The Airfield was rushing by, the concrete rumbled louder and louder under the spindly fragile wheels then it happened. Two rockets were ignited underneath the aircraft as the afterburners ignited. The roar of sheer unadulterated power permeated and shook everything. The cockpit felt like a child's rattle. Everything was moving. Within seconds the ground fell away, undercarriage hissed and clunked away and the fighter was banking hard right. Reg immediately felt the clamping of the anti G suit on his legs and arms as his head lolled involuntarily to the side.

The aircraft gained effortless rapid height Reg heard the tower speak.

"Fulcrum 2 you are clear for low level pass."

The ascending jet was now nose diving towards the Russian fields. A thought flashed through his brain that this was the moment to find God.

Dimitri pulled the MIG out of the dive and leveled out. The altimeter directly in front of Reg read 200 feet. The closeness of the ground gave a true sensation of speed; it was like riding a bullet.

"700 miles per hour Mr. Moorcroft, just subsonic" Dimitri laughed. "Don't go away."

The agile aggressive aircraft stood on its tail. The afterburners once again ignited. This time there was no rattling or earth induced vibration, just massive thrust upwards. Reg's heavy head was pinned back onto the seat as they climbed into the heavens.
Dimitri leveled out the aircraft. It was almost silent. Reg looked at the altimeter, it showed 80,000 feet.

"Twenty five kilometers or about fifteen miles." Dimitri had guessed his thoughts

"It's beautiful is it not Mr. Moorcroft?" Dimitri crackled.

Reg stared into the nearby blackness of space then at the amazing curved globe below them. Between the two on his seen horizon was a halo of glistening white.

"I don't think I can describe it Dimitri. Beautiful is insufficient"

The aircraft gently and almost in a whisper glided downwards, black space becoming once more blue sky.

"Hang on tight Mr. Moorcroft; we're going to have some fun."

The aircraft lurched upwards but this time no afterburners and very little thrust. Lift and forward movement ceased as it slid backwards on its tail towards earth, only to be elegantly flipped and recovered as engines and attitude brought back control. Spins, more spins, barrel rolls and loops bounced his weak heavy head from side to side like a broken doll. He became used to the vicious clamping of his limbs by the anti-g suit but still had problems with his brain trying to catch up with his vision as ground and sky swapped places so quickly and often. Then it was over, the undercarriage dropped down spoiling the quiet aerodynamics. The rubber speckled runway apron approached rapidly and then they were down and cruising slowly with the cockpit open towards the hard standing. Reg's oxygen mask dangled on its small black chain as he once again breathed normally.

Hot dark coffee and a ham sandwich waited for them in the pilot's room. Reg tried not to be in awe of Dimitri's skills telling himself it was simply his day job but couldn't really imagine Reg Moorcroft being able to do it. It required a certain bravado coupled with superb hand eye coordination and intelligence. A rare combination he decided.

Over the coffee Reg found out Dimitri had two children, a boy of nine and a girl of eleven. That he lived in a modern three bed roomed apartment and liked to holiday on the Black Sea. Dimitri found out his first name was Reg, and that he worked in an office.

"Would you like me to get someone to show you around Nizhny Reg?"
"No it's OK. I've got a plane to catch. Could you arrange for the black car to take me back to Nizny Airport?"
"You mean the Moskvitch?"
"If you say so." Laughed Reg.
"Sure. It'll take about half an hour."
"That's fine. It'll take me that long to get all this kit off." Dimitri stood up and shook his hand.
"Good luck with your life Reg Moorcroft."
"Thank you." Reg replied. They both knew they would never see each other again. Why would they?

Chapter 5.

Reg unlocked the door and placed the black bag down next to the telephone table.

"Is that you love?" Rosamund called out from the lounge.

"No. It's a teenage mutant Ninja Turtle, all slimy and green."

"There's some tea in the pot if you want one. I didn't expect you back until later so I haven't made you anything to eat. I can do you some tomatoes and eggs on toast if you're hungry. How was your flight?"

"The pilot flew a bit high, I can't see the need to go as high as 35,000feet coming from Edinburgh to Bristol. I would have thought 25,000 feet would have been plenty high enough. Yes, that sounds lovely. I'm famished."

"Good morning Tina."

"Hello"

"Hi Karen."

Reg ran the office gauntlet towards his office.

"Good weekend Reg? You and Rosamund do anything?" Corrallee with her bright red shiny lips offsetting her dark sleek black bob chirped up.

"No not really, quick helicopter from Staverton to The VIP desk of terminal five Heathrow, British Airways overnight flight to Moscow – first class of course. Local flight to Nizhny Novgorod then a Moskvitch limousine to Dolinsk Sokol Military air base for a flight in a MIG 29 jet fighter. Break the sound barrier then fifteen miles high to the edge of space; view the curvature of the earth and the blackness of space. A few aerobatics on the way down then Napolina plum tinned tomatoes and two poached eggs on thick Waitrose bread and Lurpak butter for Sunday tea."

"You manage to clean all your windows then Reg?" Corrallee chirped looking at her screen. Reg stopped, put down his bag and coat on the floor and walked over to her desk. He stared intently into her eyes and replied "NO".

"I reckon he's having a funny turn you know." Corrallee whispered to Karen.

"The grass 'll soon start growing now that the light nights are here, have you had the mower serviced Reg?"

"No, I'll see to it this weekend." Reg muttered from behind the Guardian.

"Rosamund?"

"Yes."

"I thought we might try somewhere different for our holidays this year. I'm getting bored with France."

"But you like France and Madame Hildegard will be very miffed if we don't take her cottage. She keeps those three weeks for us every year."

"I fancy Bermuda."

"That's a bit exotic. Can we afford it Reg?"

"Yes."

"I'm going to make a cuppa before the ten o'clock news. Do you want one?"

"Yes please."

"There you go, don't let it go cold reading that paper. You know what you're like."
Rosamund placed the white mug by his feet.

"And don't kick it over." She added.

'And finally a forty two year old woman Kathleen Thomas from Richmond in Yorkshire has died in hospital. Mrs. Thomas suffered a heart attack the day after being a victim of an armed robbery in the Richmond branch of the Yorkshire Building Society in July last year. She had remained in a coma for nine months and never regained consciousness. Yorkshire Police are now treating the robbery as murder. A forty eight year old male from Huddersfield has been arrested. Now for the local news in your area--------------------.'

Reg lowered his paper and stared at the screen.

"Going to the loo. I'll feed the cat whilst I'm up."

Rosamund raised her hand so that it brushed his arm as he walked past her.

"Thanks love."

The BANG! Sounded very close to the house. Rosamund turned off the telly and picked up Reg's cup.

"Reg are they shooting rabbits in the field behind? That sounded very close." Sophia the cat purred and brushed around her legs.

"Reg. I thought you were feeding the cat."
"Reg!"
"Reg! Where are you?"
"Yes, just coming, won't be a minute."
"What are you doing? What was that big bang? It sounded really close."
"Lampers love, over the back wall, I could hear them walking."

Reg looked up at the large hole he'd just blown in his shed roof. Through it he could see the stars. It was one of those really clear nights - 'you dont' get many of them' - he thought, 'where you could see thousands of stars.' He was glad to be alive and ashamed to be alive, all at the same time. He couldn't even top himself successfully, chickened out at the last moment. Moved the barrel a fraction and blew his shed roof to smithereens, well not quite, it was a substantial hole though, good job it was on the side away from the kitchen window.

'When you wish upon a star.
Makes no difference who you are.
When you wish upon a star,

Your dreams come true.

The ridiculous song and tune seemed to trickle into his mind through the hole. The gun lay on his workbench a tiny curl of oily smoke drifted out the end of the barrel. Quickly he hid it under his rag pile and turned out the light.

"What on earth are you doing out in your shed this time of night? Sit down and finish your tea before it gets cold."

"Thinking about a 'smart flap'"
"What on earth are you on about?"
"They're new, it's a cat flap. The cat has a special collar with a chip in it that will unlock the cat flap. Sophia's alway pestering to come into my shed when I'm in there, sometimes she sleeps on my rag pile but if I just fit an ordinary flap that brute from next door will get in and all hell will break loose."

Reg half sat, half collapsed, half slumped into the big blue chair. The TV news had moved on. Now it was the weather, some early thirties woman with an intense delivery and rather large tits. Of course she wasn't presenting the weather because of her tits. It was because she was a scientist and could talk forever.

"What happens if your dream has already come true, then what do you do?"

Rosamund looked at him as though he'd just dropped in from another planet as opposed to coming in the back door.

"What on earth are you talking about?" She said for a second time.

"Well it's a really clear night tonight and you can see thousands of stars, just made me think of that song, you know, the one that goes

'When you wish upon a star.
Makes no difference who you are.
When you wish upon a star,
Your dreams come true.'

What happens if your dream has already come true?"
"You think up another dream, now drink your tea then we'll go upstairs I'm tired."
"You go love. I'm going to wait for the ten o'clock news."
"Who sang that song?" Rosamund asked as she headed for the door.

"Jiminy Cricket in Pinocchio."

"Oh yes, how could I have possibly forgotten that! Don't forget to lock the doors and make sure the cat's in. We don't want another shrieking screaming fight like this morning. That cat next door is not nice."

"Bit like it's owner then." Reg muttered quietly enough for her to hear.

Rosamund left the room and Reg was free to think.

The comfort of the armchair seemed inappropriate for his mind, really he should be in a cream and grey cell. surrounded, encapsulated, confined, yes! Imprisoned in brick and steel, yes that's where he should be, that would sit better with his conscience.

The plan was that no one should get hurt, frightened for a short while, yes, but not hurt, not really hurt, now she was dead, the woman was dead, just as though he'd exploded her head and not the watermelon.

"Reg! Reg!" Rosamunds voice tumbled down the stairs. It had this musical cadence about it, high, low, high. It was half request, half command, Reg had no idea how she did it. Ideally she wanted him to come to her so that she could convey her instructions.

"What Dear?" He shouted from the armchair. It became obvious to Rosamond that he wasn't going to come up the stairs.

"Can you put the clothes from the washing machine into the tumble dryer before you come up? Make sure there are no woolens will you?"

"Yes dear."

'She was dead, I wonder if she had any children? She looked the type to have children. She looked like a mother, not one of these pushy business women all high heels and quick repartee. Eyebrows so sharp you'd cut your finger if you stroked them.' Reg thought to himself as he waited for 'Only Fools and Horses' to finish and the news to come on. It was over nine months now since 'it'. It seemed like a mad crazy dream. Things had changed, his office wasn't boring anymore it was 'safe' .The people he saw everyday now not moronic automatons but sensible people working for their families. The fear, excitement and terror! -Yes it was a kind of terror- of 'it' had reset his life values. Although some of her ways and habits annoyed him, there was a realization that time has it's limits, one day he wouldn't be here to be annoyed or one day she wouldn't be around to annoy him. No! He'd settle for comfortable familiarity.

The news scrolled on forever, American hostages in Tehran, What Jimmy Carter was doing about it. Some sort of Nuclear explosion at the Three Mile Island plant in Pennsylvania. It was all so far away, made even more unreal by the flickering convenience of television. You didn't feel anything watching a small screen, not like pulling a trigger, absorbing an explosion, wincing at the noise, Smelling the hot power of burnt cordite. 'Now that was real!'

'Thatcher' She dominated everything at home, trouble was you couldn't distinguish between her and 'Dame Edna' except that the latter was very funny and the former most definitely not.

"Reg. Reg, you coming up?" Her voice flew down the stairs again.

He'd have to paint the stairs soon, the paint at well used points was wearing through to dirty lower layers. It looked a mess, it annoyed him everytime he saw it and if it annoyed him it would certainly be a source of extreme annoyance to Rosamund. Twenty years ago she'd have been going on at him to do it but now she knew that he'd do it in his own good time.

"Just waiting to catch the weather love, be up in a minute." Reg reflected on his last phrase, a long time ago, when they were young he was up most nights, now it was an effort, almost a chore. He had to pretend of course. Women were complicated, it wasn't just the physical thing, it was the mental thing, "I'm still attractive! Still desirable! Still sexy!" No it was a physical confirmation of her femininity, her role within her world as a 'woman'. With a bloke it was just a shag when he felt horny. No, women were far more complicated than men.

'A forty three year old woman - Kathleen Thomas has died in hospital after failing to come out of a coma. Mrs Thomas suffered a heart attack following an armed robbery at the Yorkshire Building Society office in Richmond, relapsed into a coma and never recovered. Police are now treating the robbery as murder. A forty eight year old Huddersfield man who is already in custody for the robbery is to be further interviewed. She leaves a husband and seventeen year old daughter. And now for the weather--------
-----------------.'

Reg turned off the TV, the lights, and slowly climbed the stairs. Sofia the cat pushed against his legs with every step. 'An seventeen year old daughter. God he'd have loved a daughter, they'd tried for years, nothing had happened, they'd talked about having tests and some medical help but neither he or Rosamund had fancied that, far too intrusive. Yes he'd have spoiled her rotten if they'd had one. He wondered what her name was? How was she coping with her mother gone? He'd ruined her childhood, wrecked her life and for what? A trip to the edge of space in a fast jet. Was that worth a child's happiness? Maybe she wasn't happy before? Maybe her dad was a drunk, a philanderer with a girlfriend or two. Maybe her mom and dad were always fighting or arguing in front of her, making her cry, making her hide away in her bedroom. It wasn't his fault she relapsed into a coma, she must have had a weak heart anyway, forty two year old people don't usually have heart attacks unless there's a problem. 'Stop beating yourself up.' Reg told himself.

Reg lay back on the soft pillow in the darkness.

"How far back do you think responsibility goes? He said, half to himself, half to nobody, half to Rosamund if she was still awake.
"What are you talking about Reg? Go to sleep."
"Well what if, during the last twenty five years you got up early every morning and made me a luscious full English breakfast, you know, Walls pork sausages, fried eggs, fried bread, fried bacon, Heinz beans, a piece of fried black pudding, fried mushrooms, a fried tomato. Absolutely delicious but lot's of fat, then one day I had a heart attack and died. The coroner's report said I'd died from blocked arteries caused by excess cholesterol which in turn was caused by a fatty diet. Would you think that you'd killed me?"

There was silence as she turned over to her left side, leaving her back towards him.

"No, It'd be your fault, you could have said no thanks to the breakfast and gone out and done some exercise. You know, like you started to do months ago when you got me to dig out and wash your tracksuit."

"Ummm! I suppose you're right.!"
"Of course I'm right, I'm always right.Now, for goodness sake go to sleep."

Chapter 6.

Age was having an impact. His sleeping patterns were changing, bit's of him hurt, even in bed, causing him to toss and turn more. Rosamund got quite 'tetchy' when it disturbed her. They'd talked about separate beds but that seemed a betrayal of their relationship. Husbands and wives slept together. That's what you did.

It was Monday. He'd think of something ridiculously amusing to say to the office girls when he walked in towards his office whilst he was driving to work. 'His Office', he thought how ridiculous those words were. It wasn't his office, sure he had a key, sure nobody else used it, but it wasn't his. He stopped himself. He was doing this sort of thing far too often these days, landing on everyday words and phrases and thinking about how relevant or irrelevant to his life they were. 'For God's sake stop it.' He told himself.

"What's in my lunch box?" It was a ridiculous question. He already knew. He didn't have Superman's x-ray vision but it would be cold pork and stuffing sandwiches in Waitrose whole grain soft bread with a smattering of Lurpak butter which Rosamund didn't approve of but he insisted on. A tomato, an apple and a pot of Greek style full fat yogurt. She didn't approve of that either but the 'skinny' yogurts just tasted like cold slimy jelly.

"Just the usual." The voice descended the stairs without a person.

Rosamund was still upstairs doing whatever. Sofia purred and rubbed around his legs until he gave in and put some bits in her dish. There were 'some bits' left over from last night but she wanted fresh ones from the box. Grabbing his lunch box and his car coat he headed out of the front door.

"Byeee! See you tonight!" Reg wondered how many times he'd said that. Rosamund either didn't hear or couldn't be bothered to answer. 'I suppose it's just as tedious for her.' He thought to himself. 'What if, in the cold grey of a Monday morning, she really hated him, or just disliked him and couldn't wait for him to leave so she could relax, be herself and not - his wife.' 'No that was ridiculous, she was far too nice and loving towards him.'

The silver Honda beeped at him as he pressed. 'All Honda Civics were silver,' he thought to himself. He'd never seen a yellow one. He could almost guarantee the level of traffic on a Monday, somehow the overall expression from the drivers was one of glum resignation. 'The Glums' Ron and Ethel, The Billy Cotton Bandshow. Reg's mind flew back to his boyhood, The Goonshow, The Navy Lark, usually followed by 'Sing Something Simple' on pleasantly boring Sunday afternoons.

The Monday morning 'repartee' entry into the big office was now a requirement.

"Morning Reg, good weekend?" Was a mandatory greeting.

Reg dropped from fifty to forty as he entered the speed limit. He laughed to himself. Last week one of the young Inspectors, Julia, told him a story of how a rather strange, rather alternative Constable had dragged her out of her office, sat her in his Police car and disclosed to her his new idea for road safety by a demonstration. He'd called it 'Spot - on - Speeding'. The idea being that when you came in sight of a speed limit sign you carried on to an estimated point before the sign, then lifted off at a point where your momentum will bring you to the sign at the correct speed, without using brakes of course. The idea being to make the compliance with the speed limit a process of skill and judgement, a competition with yourself rather than the inconvenient imposition of a law. He'd thought it quite clever but Julia was of the opinion that the Constable was off his rocker so he went along with her.

"Yes thank you. Night train to Edinburgh, helicopter to Balmoral then out on the hills with Charles and Phillip, had a magnificent Imperial Stag in the crosswires of the old Mannlicher but then I sneezed and it ran off."

"Did you watch Dallas or Dynasty?" Corallee chirped from behind her typewriter.

"Both." Reg responded as he put his key into the lock of his office. He entered and looked around. Nothing had changed since Friday night. His cactus was still alive but hadn't seemed to have grown at all. These days his computer screen was thin, black and flat, not like the old days when the V.D.U.was a huge tube television type shape that dominated his desk. There was a special hole in his desk for the wires. He stood there looking into the comfortable safe office. He was a criminal, maybe a murderer, a bank robber, what was he doing here? He'd flown to the edge of space, looked into the blackness of the unknown, peered down into the blueness of the planet. How could he pretend this was OK?

"Oh Yes! I'm the Great Pretender"
Pretending that I'm doing well.
My need is such,
I pretend too much.
I'm lonely, but no one can tell."
The Platters lyrics bounced around the cream walls of his office before lodging back in his head.

He'd retire, that's what he'd do. He didn't need the money even without his ill gotten gains. The 'event' had changed him. He'd moved on, yes this was safe and comfortable but it was a sham, every word to every person a deceitful act, every click of his mouse a betrayal. Yes he'd retire. Reg placed his car coat on the hook and his lunch box on the filing cabinet in the corner. Glennys appeared with his coffee and a copy of this mornings 'Taliban Times'. She looked at him as she placed them on his desk. Somehow she could sense something. Something unsaid, unspoken, but something there nevertheless.

"Why do you read 'The Guardian' Reg?" Her eyes were looking straight into his. Deeper than his face. There was a pause, a considered silence.

"I'm really Robin Hood, or maybe William Tell or possibly even Superman! Everyday I wear red underpants and have a red cape in my briefcase. Would you like to have a look?"
"What, in your briefcase? You haven't got one Reg."
"No, my red underpants."
Reg pretended to undo the buckle of his belt as Glennys fled for the door, she turned on her way out.
"You get worse with age! You should retire!" She closed the door.

Reg sat at his desk and clicked the computer on. She was right of course, He was right. He had noticed that childish or immature things were once again becoming of interest but in a different way, as though it was a circle, you started off a child and ended up a child. 'How lovely', he thought. How lovely to feel wonder or amazement at something. A stick of rock. Now that was amazing. How on earth did they get 'Blackpool' or Skegness' to run through the whole stick? Amazing!

The computer limbered up in front of him, clicking and flashing, demanding his input, his attention. The headlines of the Guardian competed for his attention 'Saddam Seizes Power in Iraq'. When he was a boy at school it was called Mesopatania, a far more romantic name than hard short Iraq. He took a sip of his coffee, it was still too hot. There was a critical temperature, a sweet spot of heat, even more so with tea, a time when it was just right to drink it in large gulps as opposed to insipid sips. He'd leave it for a while. Trouble was if he left it too long it was too cold to drink and Glennys would be cross.
Allan Mayor tapped on Regs door and entered without waiting for a 'come in.' Allan was now a newly promoted Sargeant, keen as a newly opened pot of Colmans mustard.

"Morning Reg."
"Morning Allan. What can I do for you?"
Allan sat down without being asked in the only other seat in the small office.

"Got anything on central locking systems, there seems to be a spate of vehicle thefts, mainly new Cortinas and the like, the one thing in common is they all had these new central locking systems. Just wondered if there was anything on the system about it?"
"How's married life?" Reg asked as he tapped away.
"Fantastic, best thing I've ever done. Jenny's expecting, early days yet, due in February."
"Oh, didn't know that, you kept that quiet. Congratulations. Do you know who the father is?" Reg kept a poker straight face staring at his screen as his inappropriate joke bottomed out. They both ignored it.

"Here we go, fresh off the press from Dagenham, apparently these systems are pneumatic, operated by air."
"Yes I know what pneumatic means Reg."
"Well apparently if you cut a hole in a tennis ball, place it over the outside lock and give the ball a whack the air pressure generated is sufficient to spring the system."

Reg glanced over at Allan.

"Sorry about that Allan, one of my famous bad taste jokes. Seriously, congratulations, do you know what the baby is yet?"
"No, too early Reg, another two months before we can tell."
"What are you hoping for?"
"A girl, Shirley would like the first one to be a girl."
"Rosamund and I wanted a daughter but you know how it is, nothing happened."
"Was that an issue then Reg?" Allan sensed the deep void that was in Reg's life.
"Yes. Always there but never visited." The two men looked at each other.
"Can you do a bulletin about this Reg? If we pull any lads over with a tennis ball with a hole in it we can nick them for 'going equipped'."
"Sure, this afternoon, is that OK Allan?"
"Great, any chance it will be ready for the two o'clock parade?"
"Every chance."
"Cheers Reg. See you later."

Allan left, closing the door quietly behind him.
'For gods sake he was an armed robber, a woman had died, what the hell was he doing sitting here playing 'charades'. He'd have to get out! Retire!'

Reg knocked respectfully on Superintendent Bill Furber's door. Normally he'd just tapp, listen if there was anyone in there or if he was on the phone and then just go in but today he wanted to start the process of disassociation so waiting was appropriate.

"Come in."

Reg opened the door and entered, it was a grey and cream office the same as his only bigger, it had two windows. It could best be described as 'functional' there was nothing there to make it personal, make it 'his'. It was though there was tacit admission that his feet under that desk were temporary.

"Morning Reg, what can I do for you?" There was a sigh, as though he knew there was a problem coming his way.

Reg held the corner of the chair that was lurking in front of Bill's large desk. It wasn't directly in front of the desk, like an 'interview' chair but angled to one side like a disarmingly friendly but still professional chair.

Bill picked up on the gesture.

"Sit down Reg, Sit down. What's the problem?"

Reg thought to himself that his quiet demeanour and body language had conveyed to Bill that there was 'a problem'.

"I'm going to retire Bill."

There was a long silence as Bill assessed if he was serious or not.

"When?"
"End of the month."
"That doesn't give me much time to find a replacement, equal opps and all that."
"Get young Allan Mayor to do my job, he's always in my office, he knows roughly how the systems work, plus he's as keen as mustard."
"He's a police officer Reg, you know how things are with the current climate about officers being in quiet office jobs."
"He's a newly promoted Sargeant Bill and he's passed his Inspectors exam, and his wife is expecting. Give him six months in there whilst you advertise the job."
"Shall we have some coffee Reg?"
"That would be nice. Any biscuits?"

Bill Furber looked at him. Before pressing a button and speaking into the intercom.

"What's brought you to this?"

"I've decided I need some stimulation in my life, you know a shot of adrenalin up my arse, Been thinking about a career in bank robbery or maybe murder, a hit man or something."

Bill Furber smiled as Penelope brought in the coffee and a plate of biscuits.

"You and your stories Reg. You know your Monday morning tales are famous throughout the station. People have started writing them down, they say they're going to write a book."

"Mind if I have these two Bourbons Bill? They're my favourites."

"Go ahead, dunk if you want to. Why now?"

"I've run out of steam Bill, I simply don't care anymore and that's not good. It's as though age is resetting my ideas of what is important. A smash and grab from a petrol station isn't important to me and it should be. What is important to me is what's in my lunchbox, or what's on the telly tonight. It's time for me to go Bill."

"Don't you think we're all like that Reg, but we have a duty, a job to do. I look at these young probationers standing rigid and nervous in front of me in this office, sharp as a razor, not an ounce of fat on them, able to run up the stairs three steps at a time. When was the last time you or I ran up the stairs Reg? They're shit scared of this crown on my shoulder and when they close the door I examine myself and my faults. We all have them Reg, You're sixty five in three years time and then you'd have to go, can't you hang on till then?"

"No, I want to go now Bill plus I don't want you to tell anyone. I don't want a big card with loads of signatures and smart comments folk have had to think up. I don't want to get pissed at some back slapping do, I don't want an expensive briefcase or watch. I just want to finish work oneday, go home and never come back."

Bill Furber took some silent sips of coffee but no biscuit.

"OK Friday the twenty eighth it is then, leave your office key in here before you go." What about young Allan Mayor?"

"He'll have to know obviously, He should spend a couple of days with me before the day. Tell him a lie, tell him I'm having to retire on health grounds and that it's delicate. I don't want anyone to know and I most definitely don't want to talk about it. Swear him to secrecy."

"OK." There was a silence. "I'm going to leave it twenty four hours Reg before I put the wheels in motion. Come and see me before then if you have second thoughts If I don't see you or hear from you I'll take it as read." Bill Furber finished off his coffee and put the cup silently back in the saucer. "You know Reg we're all shit scared or bored shitless. Happiness is a very elusive thing especially when you're old and cynical. My mother died of bowel cancer, it wasn't much fun, the thing I remember her saying to me in the last few days when she was hooked up to a morphine pump was - 'Bill I don't know what I've done to deserve this.' The moment has stuck with me ever since. Of course she hadn't done anything to deserve it, she was wonderful. Everyday Reg I inspect the contents of my toilet looking for blood. As I said Reg, we're all shit scared, 'scuse the pun. Why do you really want to go Reg?"

"Things have changed Bill, I'm not the man you think I am, I've seen sights that would amaze you, been places you've never heard of, experienced sensations that only a few people on this planet have. I just can't hide in a comfortable office anymore smiling at everyone. I dont care about them, their lives, their marriages, their babies, their dogs, their holidays. I just dont care."

"Really?" Bill Furber Quizzed.
"Really." Reg Moorcroft said as he closed the office door.

Reg left Superintendent Bill Furbers office and walked to the other end of the corridor. There was a black and white formica sign on the door. 'Reginald Moorcroft - Divisional Crime Analyst -. He wondered how long it would take the handyman to screw up a new sign. What would he do with the old sign, his sign, throw it in the bin he supposed.

"Your coffee will be cold by now." Glennys shouted out from behind her typewriter.
"I'll keep it til lunch then pop it in the microwave." Reg responded.
"Disgusting! I don't know how Rosamund has put up with you for all these years."
"Who's Rosamund?" Reg asked. Glennys ignored him.

Reg looked at his screen and thought of running a voters check for Kathleen Thomas in Richmond Yorkshire, too risky, at any stage in the future it was there, indelible, hiding as a few computer bits in an ocean of gigabytes but there nevertheless. No he'd go to the library if he wanted to do it. No, he had to do it. He had to know.

Chapter 7.

Reg looked out of the window, although it was May it was still chilly. He'd put his coat on, not carry it. He took one last look. Allan Mayor's police jacket was hanging on the coat rack resplendent with his Sergeant's stripes. There was nothing to indicate that Reg Moorcroft had spent the last eighteen years of his working life in it. Locking the office he turned right heading for Bill Furber's office and not left towards the lift. Corrallee piped up.

"Eight minutes early Reg. You having a midlife crisis? Where is it this weekend, Mustique with Maggie and Roddy?"

Reg stopped and turned towards her.

"Corrallee can you give these keys to Bill Furber or Penelope if he's not in?"
"How come?"
"I don't need them anymore."
"What you talking about Reg?"
"I've retired, had enough. Too old, not interested, finished. Goodbye."
"He's having a funny turn, I've noticed he's been a bit odd recently, you know forgetting a few things, letting his coffee go cold. One day last week he came back from his usual 'eleven o'clock visit' with his flies undone. Didn't seem at all bothered when I told him." Corrallee whispered to Sarah on the next desk down."Expect they're going to upgrade his computer over the weekend."

"Actually it's Neverland, Michael has asked me over to look at his new roundabout and amuse 'bubbles' whilst he records another number one hit."

"Told you." Corrallee leaned over mouthed to Sarah, Her eyebrows raising to just below her hairline.

"Let me out Jim will you, I've left my card in the office, can't be bothered to repark and get it."
"Sure Reg." Jim Harrison searched in his wallet for the white card and pushed it into the machine, the arm obediently swung up.Of course he hadn't 'left it'. He'd put it on Allan Mayor's desk as of Monday morning.
"Cheers Jim, have a good weekend." Reg eased the Civic out of the car park for the last time 'He'd get a new car,' He thought to himself, He was bored with his boring sensible Civic.

The drive out of Hereford just didn't register. The fact that a door had closed on the biggest, longest, most significant episode of his life seemed totally unreal. He knew that in six months' time if he went to the Police Station, that building he'd just spent his last eighteen years in, they would ask who he was and what he wanted - Sir!

"I've decided to change the car."
"Oh have you dear, move the cat out of your place, you know how she likes to sit in your place, she'll cover it in hairs. Fish fingers, mash, peas and a tomato, is that OK for tea?"
"Yes, it's a green one, a dark green."
"I thought you liked silver?"
"I'm bored with it, every other car you see is silver. It's a Vauxhall."
"Isn't that a bit of a come down from our Honda Civic Reg?"
"It's a special one, a special edition. They've named it after a flower."
"Well it sounds nice I'm not sure I'm too keen on dark green though. Is it bigger or smaller than the Civic? Drink your tea before it gets cold. Shall I put the news on?"
"Yes OK, it's bigger. It's called a 'Lotus Carlton',"
"It sounds like an exotic tropical hotel. Do we really need a bigger car Reg?"
"No we don't need anything Rosamund, I just liked it so I thought 'Why not?'"
"Can we afford it Reg? You'll be retiring in a few years so we need to be careful."
"I'm not retiring in a few years Rosamund."
"Oh for goodness sake Reg, you can't go on after sixty five. It's just too much for you."
"You don't understand dear. I've retired now, finished today, handed in my keys, never going back."

Rosamund stood up from the TV and looked at him.

"You're joking me?" Slipping back into the Essex vernacular of her youth.
"No, Had enough of everything, people, computers, cream painted toilets, cream painted offices, cream painted stairs. I decided one day they would paint me cream and no one would see me. I wouldn't exist. I need time for me Rosamund."

Rosamund sat down on the other end of the sofa. Reg could sense her brain whizzing round in panic mode. There was a silent few minutes as she pretended to watch the news.

"What are you going to do Reg? Spend your days in the shed?"
"No, I'm going to travel about."
"What do you mean? Travel about."
"I'm going to get in my new car and travel about, there are loads of places I've never seen or been to. I'm going to go to Bakewell and eat a bakewell tart. I'm going to go to Chelsea and eat a bun, to Scotland and eat a pie, to Cornwall and eat a pasty. I'm going

to dig out my old Kodak Brownie, you know the one my Aunty gave me after I'd passed the eleven plus, and wherever I visit take a black and white photo and write a poem"

"You'll get fat."

"You could come with me and help me get fat." Reg knew she'd refuse.

"No thanks, you know travelling upsets my tummy."

"Why didn't you tell me you were going to retire, are they having a 'do' for you?"

"No, nobody knows except Bil Furber and Allan Mayor, he's going to be doing my job for a while. Oh and I told Corrallee on the way out but she didn't believe me."

"I have to admit Reg, I'm having problems believing you. It's just not like you to do this sort of thing."

"We all have a secret self Rosamund, there are things you keep secret from me and we've been together for forty two years."

"No there aren't."

"Yes there are, you were a terrible flirt when we were young, when your bottom was the cutest bottom in town." Reg laughed.

Rosamund lowered her eyelids and smiled.

"That was a long time ago Reg, I didn't think you noticed."

"Do you want me to name them?"

"No it's OK."

"As I said Rosamund, we all have our secret self."

"When are you getting the new car?

"Next Monday."

"How much was it love, have you part exchanged it?"

"Yes they did me a good deal, gave me three thousand for the Civic."

"That sounds good, how much will you have to pay then?"

"Forty five thousand pounds."

Rosamund stopped in her tracks or rather froze on her end of the sofa.

"That's more than all our savings Reg. What are you doing? Are you having some sort of breakdown, a crisis? A brand new Honda Civic is only about ten thousand pounds."

"I had an insurance policy mature, it's with the Police Mutual, a work thing, had it for twenty five years, the subs just went out of my pay automatically, I'd forgotten about it to be honest." Reg lied.

"And you've spent it all on a dark green Vauxhall car?"

"Yes."

"I'll get your tea."

Rosamund rose up off the Sofa and went into the kitchen. Sophia the cat immediately leapt into her place. She stood in the kitchen for a moment. It was as though everything was as it should be but there was a bomb coming through the ceiling. She looked at Reg's empty lunch box on the work surface and wondered if he'd ever need it again. He certainly wouldn't need it on Monday. She pulled out the grill just in time, Reg hated over cooked fish fingers, he preferred them lightly fried but she refused to cook them like that because of the fat. She carried his meal through on a tray and silently gave it to him. Like her, he was pretending to be engrossed in the news but really he was somewhere else.

It was three in the morning, Reg's ever expanding prostate usually only gave him two to three hours sleep before a trip to the bathroom. Rosamund was by now used to his nocturnal wanderings. He'd been to the doctors, had his blood checked and a finger up his bum and everything was OK it wasn't cancer. The doctor lied though, he said it wouldn't hurt but a rigid gloved finger suddenly thrust up your arse most definitely did hurt.

Slipping quietly out of the back door he entered the blackness of his shed. He didn't need a light, he'd prepared everything. Quickly he rummaged under the pile of rags for the Waitrose carrier bag and it's carefully counted contents of forty five thousand pounds. Most were fifty pound notes but some were twenty pound notes. Reg crammed the bag quickly into his black rucksack, closed the shed door and went back in, hanging his bag on the coat hooks where it normally lived. Sophia pestered around his legs for food. Reg ignored her, went upstairs and flushed the toilet.

It was his first 'retired' Monday, he could tell Rosamund wasn't at all happy with the change in routine. Normally she'd go downstairs, feed the cat, check the washing machine and dryer, pack his lunch box, then go back upstairs with a cup of tea for them both. Today the lunchbox was redundant, it sat in the cupboard, washed, clean and dry, unused, not required. She felt like the lunchbox. Reg waited for her to go shopping. He knew where she was going and what she was going to buy. Two pork pies from Hancock's the butchers, some cherry tomatoes from Marks and Sparks, then odds and ends from Waitrose. He went to put on his car coat as it was a cold drizzly morning, stopped, looked at it then changed his mind. He hated everything it represented. It wasn't him anymore, bank robbers didn't wear car coats, he'd manage in his jumper, go to Cheltenham in his new car and buy a leather jacket.

The radio in the Civic was stuck on two channels, Radio Wyvern for when he was in a good mood and could tolerate mindless adverts or BBC Hereford and Worcester for when he needed to know about the traffic at Harewood End, Lienthall Starkes or wherever. Halfway along the M50 the signal inevitably faded until you moved towards Worcester. At the junction with the M5 he turned it off. The Civic was immaculate, whoever eventually bought it would have a bargain. EvansHalshaw was the biggest Vauxhall dealer in Birmingham. Reg put his hand on the black rucksack resting on the front passenger seat, it sent his mind back to Richmond, to the sound of that huge explosion in the building society, to the quivering, then nameless woman who sat in the chair as he lifted and fired the gun. Now she had a name, now she was dead. What had he done?

The motorway rumbled on.

It was there, on a slowly rotating turntable illuminated by spotlights. Low, dark and mean, the front end was a thinly disguised snow plough, the sides skirted and badged with the round green and cream Lotus badge tucked low behind the front wheel, the back, a boot mounted wing that frightened small children, the aluminium wheels wide and sharp.

"Is that mine?' Reg asked the young salesman who was leading him.
"No Sir, yours is in the service area having final checks and number plates fitted." The young man walked quickly with seemingly no effort at all, Reg had to lengthen his stride to keep up.
"How do you want to pay Sir?" the salesman asked as they walked around the side of the showroom.
"Cash." The Salesman stopped.
"You have forty five thousand pounds with you in cash?"
"Yes." He took a deep breath.
"Right." There was a pause. "I think we need to go to our office first, they might have a problem with disclosure, you know, where did you get that amount of cash from. Make sure you're not a bank robber, that sort of thing." They both laughed.
"Under the mattress if you know what I mean." Reg winked at the young sharply dressed man. "Don't like the tax man taking my money. There's forty five thousand and two hundred pounds in the Waitrose bag in my rucksack, just to help you get over any 'problems'."
"I'm sure we can help with that Sir, this way please."

Reg slipped behind the thick large steering wheel into the leather armchair that served as a driver's seat. In front of him was a large round speedo calibrated to one hundred and eighty miles per hour, under his left hand were six forward gears and one reverse. The clutch pedal required so much pressure it was for men with weight lifters thighs. It made the Civic feel like a toy. He eased it into first gear and slowly moved out into the late morning light. His rucksack was empty, his wallet full, He'd head for Cheltenham just to get used to driving it and have a look for a leather jacket. This wasn't a car for Reg Moorcroft, this was a car for Leo Thrust. It was mobile power, the fastest car on the road today anywhere in the UK, one hundred and seventy six miles per hour. Unbelievable! Only Leo Thrust could drive such a dangerous machine.

The boring rumbling M5 motorway was now a playground as he effortlessly and relentlessly hunted down slow BMW's and Merc's. God, it was his gun on four wheels, it had a radio but he didn't turn it on. The concentration required to drive the green car took over his mind, taking away all his regrets and doubts. He was Leo Thrust looking down on all lesser mortals struggling and floundering in the ocean of mediocre slowness below him. It seemed only a matter of blurred minutes before he was slipping left for Cheltenham.

He liked Cheltenham, it was so pretentious, so pretend, so up itself, if there was nuclear armageddon Cheltenham would survive as a bastion of Britishness. That was, of course, as long as you had money. If you were poor you weren't allowed into Cheltenham. He parked at a meter between a Maserati and a Citroen Deux Chevaux, both essential vehicles for Cheltenham. Stepping out of the Lotus he once again became Reg. Leo refused to get out. He imagined both of the cars chatting and slagging off his new money brute force interloper.

Reginald Geoffrey Moorcroft felt quite comfortable in the clothes he was wearing, fawn slacks, a cream check shirt with a white Marks and Spencers sleeveless vest underneath it, a dark green knitted tie topped with a grey pullover. Very dark green Hush Puppies, 'almost the same colour as the Lotus', he thought to himself. They all worked well with his tan coloured car coat. He liked wearing hats but they just didn't seem to go with his style of dressing. He pondered on that thought. 'Leo Thrust wouldn't be seen dead looking like that. In fact you might as well be dead 'cause nobody notices you. The only time you register with anyone is when you're handing over money for something.'

The shops were always changing in Cheltenham, he only visited about twice a year usually before the summer holidays to get something new for France or at Christmas time to get something for Rosamund. Sometimes he'd pop into a trendy pub and have a tall glass of expensive lager. He felt uncomfortable and out of place in the 'hip' place but liked to feel the alcohol releasing his inhibitions and expanding his thoughts. On the good side It helped him to choose something nice for Rosamund, on the bad side it made him wish he was buying for his daughter, searching the shops for something to make her look even more beautiful than she already was. If they'd had one he'd have called her Betty after his mum. He'd have spoilt her rotten.

'REIS'. Reg stopped and looked. 'Closing Down Sale' was plastered all over the windows. Not a shop he'd normally go in but normal was dull and boring. He knew it, he'd been normal all his life.

Two stick thin young men looked at him as he browsed the rails. He wasn't the usual 'clientele' so he may be a shoplifter. They watched him carefully. At the back of the shop
Was a rail of leather jackets, Reg thumbed through them, none of them appealed, all thin and black with chrome badges then there it was. He knew it was the one immediately. He knew it would fit perfectly.

"Can I try this on?" The stick thin youth looked quizzically at him before responding. Reg noticed he had one earring, and the remnants of a tattoo creeping up his neck.
"Yes Sir, certainly Sir. Are you considering the coat for yourself or is it a gift?"
"For me." The youth glanced disparagingly over at his colleague, his partner, his mate, his lover. Reg had yet to decide.
"It's a Belstaff, quite expensive Sir but the best quality, modelled on their traditional motorcycle jacket design, as you can see it's lined with Burberry material. Quite a heavy jacket but beautifully made."

He was right, the pockets, the flaps, the press studs, the belt, they all looked as though they were made to last. The coat itself was high quality brown leather.

"Is it in your 'Sale'?" Reg asked.
"Yes Sir, an absolute bargain, down from five hundred pounds to three hundred."

Reg slipped the heavy coat on. He was right again, it was heavy but once on it felt like a suit of armour. He felt invincible. He looked in the full length mirror, somehow he looked taller, bigger. 'Perhaps it was a trick mirror to make you look and feel good.' He thought to himself. But he did look good and he felt good.

"If I may say so Sir, that genre of jacket doesn't really go with your style of dress."
"I know, I'm going to change that. I'll take the jacket."
"In that case Sir, we have some really nice Levis jeans upstairs in large sizes. They're in the sale too."
"Would you recommend jeans with this type of jacket?"
"It's a must, Sir. anything else would be a fashion 'faux pas'.
"How about shirts."
"We don't have many Sir, but there are some very nice deep red check lumberjack type shirts in large sizes. They're upstairs as well, most of our customers are young so the

larger sizes tend to be the last to go. If you like them I would suggest a waistcoat to replace your pullover, there are some plain tan waistcoats up there in a rough serge material."

The boy and Reg climbed the stairs together.

"Shame about the shoes." By now he'd grown confident enough to drop the 'Sir'. "The clothes and jacket look great on you but you can't wear those shoes."
"Ummm I see what you mean." Reg liked what he saw in the mirror. "What do you recommend?"
"Clinkards in Montpellier Row, five minutes walk from here. They have some really sharp black leather brogues with brown heels and soles, a perfect match for jeans."

Reg bought the jacket, three shirts and two pairs of jeans.

"That will be four hundred and sixty two pounds Sir, how do you wish to pay? Cheque? We accept cheques with a bankers card."
"No, cash."
"Cash?" Repeated the young man.
"Cash." Repeated Reg.

Reg really wanted to wear his new clothes but as the boy had said, it was a no go with his shoes. He walked towards Montpelier. It was a cool greyish day, the people were an exact match with the place, elegant, tastefully expensively conservative. If you were middle aged, 'George Melly' hats almost 'de rigueur' for the following husbands. Young folk were tastefully extreme in an - 'I'm an interesting individual' sort of way. The power players - women - were absolutely committed to looking non-competitive whilst really being ultra competitive. He was glad he was a man, even if, at the moment, as he walked up the slight incline, he was indistinguishable from the sandstone facades of the bijoux shops.

The shoes came, as the boy said, they were sharp. They were black leather brogues that you didn't polish too much. You didn't want to be seen as materialistic so the shoes should be just slightly scruffy as though you didn't know their price. The shoe shop didn't have a changing facility so he was still Reg. Reg who was now in search of a hat. The rather condescending forty plus something man in Clinkards had reluctantly recommended Cotswold Country Hats in Regents Arcade. It was as though recommending any other place in which to spend money was tantamount to treason for which he could be hanged by his pompous perfect manager, who, without doubt was military, not an Officer obviously, Officers are customers, but a Sargeant Major.

Reg enjoyed walking in Cheltenham, there was always something going on, a busker, two high schoolgirls playing violin duets, a statue man, a clown come juggler, they came out with the sun and disappeared with the rain. Regents Arcade was famous for it's Wishing Fish' clock, it was very tall and complex. He'd never seen it before, it was childlike in its figurines and animals but in reality almost a miracle of engineering, a chronological masterpiece. Cotswold Country hats supplied a greenish check tweed cap and a curtained off area for customers to pose.

Reg Moorcroft went behind the curtain but Leo Thrust came out. The pristine correct staff just stared. Leo didn't care, all he cared about was, what was the best angle to wear his cap. He paid over eighteen pounds from the obviously large bankroll in his leather jacket pocket and left with Reg in the thick upmarket carrier bags. The hard leather heels of the Loakes brogues clicked confidently on the pavement, He now fitted in with Cheltenham. The nondescript observed him. Putting him down as an obscure writer who would become world famous after his death, rather like Vincent van Gogh.

'I could have told you Leo,
This world was never made for one so beautiful as you.'

Both Reg and Leo chuckled at his distortion of the Don Maclean classic as the Lotus came into sight. 'God it looked brutal. It would snarl at anyone who touched it. Except Leo of course, Leo was it's master.' He wondered if he should take the cap off in the car but decided to keep it on. He wondered before starting the engine if it was going to be a 'Starry Starry Night'. He wondered what Rosamund would say and think when she saw the new car and met Leo. The 'whoooosh' of the turbo chargers as he started the engine erased his thoughts.

He parked the car on his drive and sat in it for a moment, letting everything calm down. Reg was on the back seat hiding in three large carrier bags.

"Is that you love? Be down in a minute just doing my 'roots'."

Rosamond was fastidious about her hair, she was naturally auburn but had been stoically fighting a battle with nature for at least ten years. She hated two-tone hair where the grey roots were visible.

"Put the kettle on love. Haven't had a cup of tea since you left, been on the phone to mother for ages. She's losing her marbles you know, she's still in her twenties living in Uganda with servants."

"That's because she liked the 'colonial' lifestyle and all the kudos that went with it. Thank God she hasn't got a bean, if she had a few bob she'd be insufferable." Rosamund didn't reply. Reg clicked the telly on 'Waiting for God', 'One foot in the Grave', 'Last of the Summer Wine'. 'What a totally depressing lineup,' Reg thought, ' thank god for Blankety Blank, at least Les Dawson was reasonably funny.'

Rosamund entered the lounge and froze. Reg, AKA Leo, had deliberately not taken off his cap and coat. There was a very long silence as she looked at him.

"Well, do you like my new look?" Reg asked.
"Did you get it?" She asked, speechless in respect of his clothes.
"Yes."
"You've really handed over fortyfive thousand pounds of our money for a dark green Vauxhall car named after a flower?"
"Yes, do you want to see it? Have a go in it?"
"No thank you. What do you look like Reg? If you were a woman I'd describe you as 'Mutton dressed as Lamb', but I don't think there's an equivalent for a middle aged to old aged man."
"Yes, but if you didn't know me and you saw me shopping in Waitrose would you notice me?"
"I certainly would. I'd think what an old prat, for gods sake grow up."
"That's good enough for me, at least I wouldn't be invisible. I'll make the tea."

They sat on the blue sofa watching the TV. After all the years of closeness there was now space between them. Rosamund and Reg could sense it. It wasn't the frostiness of argumentative silence, joint sulking, not wanting to give way. No this was something different, a sense that something was missing in their lives, in their relationship. Work usually filled the void, a lunch box to make, clothes to iron but now there was no work. They had nothing to fill the hole.

"What are you going to do tomorrow? I'm not sure you've really retired, is it a prank? Shall I do your lunch box?"
"Rosamund I've retired, look at me I'm wearing retired old man's clothes, they wouldn't let me anywhere near the police station looking like this never mind in it."
"You look ridiculous, you'll be dying your hair next and going to a gym, you know, joining all those peacocks that look in full length mirrors as they lift lumps of metal."

Reg had never heard Rosamund be so incisive and cutting before.

"I'm going to Bakewell, just to look, take a few black and white photos with my Brownie, stay for a few days to get the feel of the place, write a letter, an essay, or maybe a poem about the place then come home. Oh, and try a Bakewell tart actually made in Bakewell. Expect I'll be back Thursday or Friday."

"I think you're having some sort of breakdown Reg. Shouldn't you go and see a doctor, maybe you're depressed, apparently it's quite common in elderly people."

"I'm not elderly Rosamund and I'm not depressed, in fact I know exactly what I'm doing and why I'm doing it. You can come with me if you want? The change of scenery might do you good, open your eyes to the world out there."

"No thank you. I know what's out there and it's not pleasant. What time are you setting off?"

"Normal time, about eight."

"Do you want me to pack you some sandwiches?"

"That would be nice."

"It's a joke isn't it, a trick, you're winding me up?"

Reg turned on the sofa to look at his wife. Their eyes met and looked into each other's soul.

"Rosamund -

I'm not the man they think I am at home! Oh no no no, I'm a Rocket Man!"

Reg quoted Elton John but he wasn't smiling.

"You need to see a doctor. I'll pack your sandwiches."

Rosamund peeped from behind the upstairs bedroom window curtain as a strange man left the house and headed for a dark green brute of a car. Things down the side, things on the boot, an ugly front, badges everywhere. Whatever was he doing spending all that money on that? The man was wearing blue jeans, a dark blue and red checked shirt and a brown leather jacket with a loose belt dangling. He was carrying a small bag that didn't really go with his outfit. On his head was a check peaked cap. He was right. She would notice him. She'd be intrigued and wonder who he was. The car started up, slid confidently backwards down the drive and drove off. Even that was different. In the Civic Reg would drive off carefully and slowly, as though he didn't want to go at all but today he moved off swiftly as though the car was as excited as Reg.

Leo knew the way to Derby, he'd joined the Navy as a boy from the Derby recruiting office when mum and dad lived at Borrowash but after that he wasn't sure. He'd stop at a garage, fill up and buy a map. One of those big books so he wouldn't have to put his glasses on. Leo shouldn't wear glasses, maybe he'd look into contact lenses. The Lotus was happy cantering somewhere between ninety and a hundred miles per hour. He had to reign it in to cruise with the 'legals' at just over seventy, a momentary lack of concentration and the speedo would creep up. Leo pushed Roxy Music's Avalon into the player.

'More than this - you know there's nothing!
As free as the wind,
Hopefully learning,
Why the sea on the tide,
Has no way of turning.

The lyrics seemed to fit his mood and moment perfectly. He looked at the lunch box she'd packed for him. Secretly hoping he was going to Hereford Police Station and not the Derbyshire Dales. He knew what was in it, he'd skipped breakfast, Leo Thrust would be lean and mean, but Reg had a comfortable midriff which now didn't fit. No, it would have to go, 'just eat less', he said to himself.

He stopped for fuel somewhere north of Spaghetti Junction, heading for Litchfield. The day was getting greyer and colder as he sped north. As he queued to pay for his petrol and map a smartly dressed middle aged woman glanced at him, it took a fraction of a second as their eyes scanned. She noticed him and he noticed that she had noticed. It had been a long time since that had happened. As he walked towards the car he wondered if she was looking at him, wondering who he was? Where he was going? What was he doing? If he'd walked back to his silver Civic she'd have discounted him as a crass charlatan but he wasn't, he was walking back to a Lotus Carlton, the fastest car on the road.

The moment was gone, forgotten, as Leo pressed the really heavy clutch pedal and headed up the A38 to Derby. Burton-on-Trent smelt of hops barley and Marmite, maybe he'd visit there one day, it looked unpretentious and conservative but with the hidden secret of several famous breweries. An immaculate cherished E type Jag blocked his way in the fast lane of the dual carriageway, he sat behind it, wondered if he should flash his headlights but decided against it. It took about two miles for the E type driver to feel the pressure from behind, when he did move over Leo caressed the accelerator pedal causing the large saloon to effortlessly waft past the ageing bright red sports car. The driver waved as the Carlton exceeded a hundred miles an hour. Looking at the speedo it seemed so insignificant compared to breaking the sound barrier in a MIG 29 fighter jet. The woman in the petrol station would never have guessed he'd done that. Nobody would.

It was eleven twenty when Leo stopped the car on a small grass verge in front of the white and black road sign saying 'Bakewell'. He took out his Brownie camera from it's brown canvas bag and snapped a picture. The strap was about to give in to age but the inside flap still bore his biroed in name and his boyhood address. It was the first time he'd used it in about forty plus years. It clicked as he pressed the cream plastic button then he had to wind the film on. It took him back to that day his Aunt Connie had made a surprise visit to their small street house with a gift. He'd been amazed that anyone would give him 'a gift' when it wasn't Christmas or his Birthday. She'd told him it was for passing the eleven plus. The concept of a reward for an achievement had never occurred to him, in fact his mom and dad were none too pleased when he passed as they'd have to buy him a uniform and stuff. All that 'stuff' was for posh people.

Opening the lunch box he found four sandwiches, two egg and cress, two cornbeef and tomato, a yogurt, an apple and a note - 'Drive safely, have a nice trip - Love Rosamund.' The note yanked him back to reality, he folded it up and put it in Reg's wallet. 'He'd find a nice spot to eat his lunch then find a hotel.' Leo thought as the clicking ticking cooling engine was forced back into life. The chilly grey was now breaking up as the brisk breeze let the sun through in places.

The old stone bridge was the place for lunch, or rather the riverbank nearby where he could look at it. Five solid stone arches, most of the buildings he'd seen so far seemed to be made of the same stone. This was the place to ponder a poem. He used to write poems in his youth; lots of them in a large exercise book, but he'd lost the book. 'Which was good,' he thought to himself, 'they wouldn't have really fitted in with his life. 'He'd find a nice hotel and maybe walk back here tomorrow if the weather was good.'

The sandwiches were good. Although they were exactly the same as when he was in the Police Station, somehow they tasted different, more intense, more tasty. It made him think of her. They'd met at a disco, he was with his friend Dudley, they were both drunk but still functioning. 'It's funny how the importance of the circumstances surrounding you makes you OK even after five or six pints.' Leo's thoughts meandered off. They were taking it in turns to dance with the ugly one. There always was an ugly one. Rosamund was the pretty one but it was Leo's turn to dance with the ugly one. He chuckled to himself as he remembered how he'd begged Dudley to dance with the pretty one out of turn. The rest is history, as they say. No children though, that was a bit of a disappointment, well, more than a bit. He finished the last sandwich staring at the stout immoveable resilient bridge and wondered about the men who had built it. It would be men, no machines then.

'Apple first or Yogurt?' Leo rummaged in the glove box for a tape. 'Bridge over Troubled Waters, Simon and Garfunkel,' how apt Leo thought. The large glove box of the Carlton had more than twenty cassettes in there. Leo wondered if it was fate.

'When you're weary, feeling small,
When tears are in your eyes I will dry them all.'

It made him wonder about Kathleen Thomas and her daughter, were there tears in her eyes when she died? Of course there would be. Had he caused those tears? Yes he had, of course he had, he could make up excuses, she must have had a pre-existing heart condition, you don't normally go into a coma after a heart attack, it was a wednesday, it was hot. Whatever reasons he logically applied, the circle always came back to him. Leo opened the yogurt. Greek style vanilla, his favourite, Rosamund always packed a disposable plastic spoon in his box. 'Yes, he'd come back to this spot to write a poem. If it was sunny and dry there was a bench under a willow tree. Ducks wandered the bank, quacking and shitting demanding anything you had they could eat.

The Rutland Hotel faced resolutely out onto the main square. It wasn't really a square, it was round with a small traffic island in the middle sprouting a tall supposedly very ancient cross. It was obviously used as the town's cenotaph as the remains of 'Poppy' wreaths slowly decomposed on the granite steps leading up to the cross.

"Yes Sir, can I help you?." She was about forty, thin with immaculate teeth and reddish hair in a careful 'bob'. Reg could see she was assessing him. He'd left Leo in the car but his clothes came with him and presented her with a conundrum.

"Hi, good afternoon. I'd like a room for the night please, or possibly two nights?"

His quiet voice somehow didn't match with his clothes, his style, his demeanour, somehow something didn't match. She was unsure of where to pitch the conversation.

"Front room or back?" She had blue eyes, 'if she'd been an animal she'd have been a gazelle.' Reg thought. 'Fast, yet tantalisingly gentle, nibbling at life.'
"Front please."
"They're more expensive."
"That's OK?"
"Single or double?"

"There's only one of me."

She paused and looked at his clothes. By now Reg had got used to wearing the heavy leather jacket with aplomb, using it to boost his confidence.

"I bet there is." She smiled as she reached for a key.

"How are you going to pay?"

"Cash."

"In that case I'll need a ten pound deposit."

Reg reached into the large right hand pocket of the jacket and pulled out a roll of notes. He peeled off a ten pound note and handed it over. She could have taken it without their hands touching but she didn't.

"Do you have a car?"

"Yes, it's a green Vauxhall, I've parked it around the back."

"What's the registration number?"

"I've no idea, it's new and I haven't remembered it yet."

She looked up at him.

"I'd have had you down as something more sporty, a Jag, perhaps an Alvis, something fast."

"Where's the best place for a tart?" Reg was deliberately provocative. He was quite expecting to say 'The Rutland Hotel about ten o'clock tonight'.

She looked at him smiling.

"The Bakewell Tart Shop in Matlock Street."

"OK thanks, where's my room?"

She took the key back off him.

"Follow me."

Reg followed her trim bottom enclosed in a tight grey skirt with no sign of a panty line, up the rather narrow carpeted stairs to the first floor. Turning right she led the way to the end room, put the key in the lock and opened the door for him.

"There you go Mr. Moorcroft I hope you'll be comfortable, there's double glazing so the noise should be OK."

"Thank you errrrr------." Reg fished for a name.

"Bannister. Ms Bannister." There was a pause - "Divorced." She answered his unspoken question before leaving him.

Reg wanted to shout after her - "It's not Moorcroft, it's Thrust. Leo Thrust and what time are you free tonight?" But he didn't. He'd never actually considered being unfaithful to Rosamund. He'd always hidden behind his mundaneness, his features blended in with blandness but now it was different, he was older, his face was thinner with deep interesting crags and grooves, the clothes and hat changed him into a resting tiger who's blank ferocious eyes took in everything. Evenso, if there was an opportunity he didn't think he could actually do it. He'd never be able to face her again. Leo could, but Reg couldn't.

The bed was big and comfortable, the room was a tad gaudy and gay with a huge deep purple velvet studded bed head and pale lilac wallpaper. The two large newly double glazed windows gave a view over the silent circulating traffic. He took off his jacket and shoes before surrendering to the comfort of the bed. He consciously let his facial muscles relax, letting his face and mouth drop. It always worked if he wanted to sleep.

It was two thirty when he woke, it took a few seconds to register where he was.

"Where's the Library Ms. Bannister?" Reg asked as he passed over his key. She looked surprised that he'd remembered her name. She was a middle aged nondescript divorcee, people didn't remember her name. She still had a nice figure though, 'he must have noticed it,' she thought to herself.

"Granby Road, turn right, second on the left."
"And the 'tart shop'?" They both smiled at the unspoken innuendo.
"Over the island, keep going straight, it's on your right."

He didn't really want to go towards the library. Who knows where it would lead him but he had to do something.

It was quite nice now, more sun than showers. He loved the quietly confident clunk his stylish expensive heels made on the pavement.They wouldn't last long, maybe six months before they'd need to be reheeled, there was no effort made as to longevity, it was just plain and simple quality style.

The entrance looked like a corner shop. Dark green with a small canopy over the door. The plump middle aged woman did look like a librarian.

"Could you tell me where you keep the public documents and publications?"
"What do you want?" She peered almost suspiciously over her pinkish glasses.
"Voters lists."
"First floor first door on the right. Members card?"
"I'm not a member."

Now she was suspicious.

"There's a fee."
"What, to access a public document that I've already paid for with my taxes?"
"It's kept in a warm dry heated room. There's a fee."
"How much?"
"Fifty pence."

Reg dug deep into his jeans pocket for the coin. Jeans were OK but the pockets were small and difficult to rummage about in. He handed over the coin.

"Do you want a receipt?"
"No thanks."

He'd thought about it before. Before he'd retired. It would have only taken the pressing of a few computer buttons to get it but it would leave a trace, a trail, a record, a bit like a snail on a cold morning, the snail was long gone but his mark was indelible silver.

It was just a dirty cream, rather elderly computer. There was no password, just a menu. Reg clicked on 'Voters lists.' then North Yorkshire, then Richmond, then Thomas. There were lots of them. Twenty six Thomas's in Richmondshire. Reg thought to himself that he didn't even know there was a Richmondshire District.

There she was. Kathleen Thomas, there was only one Kathleen so it had to be her. Above her name was David Alwin Thomas, below her name was Frank Kevin Thomas. Reg guessed that she would have chosen a David over a Frank. He wrote both addresses down in pencil on a notelet. Sixteen Frances Road if it was David and Kathleen. Thirty two Quakers lane if it was Frank and Kathleen. The last address took him back to his father who really liked porridge but was very fussy about it. He always insisted that mother couldn't make it properly. He cooked it in water, poured it onto a plate rather like a thick pancake, added salt and then cold milk that encircled the porridge like a moat. It was a standing family joke how Harry fussed over his porridge. He liked everything Scottish. Dad was long gone, Reg really regretted not talking to him. Sure they talked about everyday things and fishing, but not important stuff like how he met mom? Was it love at first sight? Why was he an only child? Reg put the notelet inside the peak of his cap and left.

"Got what you want?" Pink glasses asked.
"Yes thanks."
"You were quick."

"I'm good with computers, didn't want to overstay my fifty pence." Reg replied as he headed for the green door.

She ignored him.

'Now for a tart'. Reg thought as he pulled down the peak of his cap against the fickle breeze and headed for the square.

The tart shop was smaller than he expected, painted a sort of blueish, greyish purplish colour. It was nice inside. One side was taken up with display counters and serving counters, the other side was a row of white tables and chairs. Two old women sat at the end table. He thought to himself how he had perceived them. Two old women! He was undoubtedly the same age as them if not older. He wondered if they'd noticed him. 'Did you see what that old man's wearing? Which one? The one that's just come in, the one that looks like a cowboy. Yes I did notice him.' He imagined their conversation.

Reg asked for a sausage roll, a large piece of Bakewell tart and a large coffee. The woman behind the counter took his five pound note, gave him the change and told him to sit down as she would bring it over. 'Bringing it over would require at least four steps'. Reg thought. She could just call quietly to him and he would stand up and get it. It would be nice though to have her bring it over. She was early thirties, no wedding ring, in fact no jewelry at all. She wasn't ugly or pretty, she wasn't fat or thin. Reg said thank you as she placed things before him.

The sausage roll was warm and delicious, 'you should never eat sausage rolls at home, they always tasted better out.' He thought, taking a first sip of his coffee. Then after a short break to rest his taste buds he took the first portion of the tart. It was everything they said it was.

There was no such thing as 'nightlife' in Bakewell, not that Reg wanted one. He lay on his bed and considered ringing Rosamund but decided against it, he didn't want to set a precedent of 'reporting in', no, he was free, answering to no one, he quite liked it. He switched on the TV in his room and settled down to watch 'Keeping up Appearances' Rosamund was nothing like Mrs Bucket.

The next day started with a rather nice breakfast in the hotel, poached eggs and Arbroath Smokies followed by toast and marmalade with a choice of morning tea or coffee. The weather was the same as yesterday - variable.

"Will you be staying another night Sir?" Ms. Bannister asked as he handed over the key. "Oh yes, can't pass up another chance to have a tart." By now the duplicitous banter was being played out on both sides.

"I take it you enjoyed your last tart then." She smirked.

"Immensely, Ms, Bannister, and it's Reg, not Sir, the Queen has yet to anoint me."

"I think 'anoint' is the wrong word - Reg."

"Maybe, but anoint sounds far more enjoyable than accolade."

She smiled as she turned away to put his key in the box.

It was a 'chocolate box' town, mellow stone houses, cottages, pubs and shops clustered around the ancient many-times-rebuilt 'All Saints Church'. It offered it's spire as a rocket to heaven, but only for the faithful. Reg had never really taken to religion. Rosamund was far more devout than he was. Perhaps he'd write his poem about the church, or maybe the river with it's five arched gothic bridge. He was quite interested in the process of religion, mass belief in something with absolutely no evidence other than a few bits of scroll and books written by men long after the event. If he was younger he'd do Theology at Lampeter. He loved the sound of the name - Lampeter- it was wet and deeply Welsh. He'd visit Lampeter next week and have a look. Then he'd head for Richmond the week after. He often wondered how millions of humans totally believed in religion A and millions of other humans totally believed in religion B. How did that work? What about the Egyptians, they implicitly believed in the sun as a god. How did that work? There was the tart shop, just across the road. He'd have two sausage rolls and another large piece of tart with a mug of strong hot tea for lunch. If it was the same woman he'd ask her what her name was.

Full of Emily's sausage rolls and tart Reg relaxed on a bench, under a willow tree not far from the bridge. It was chilly. He zipped up the stout brass zip on his leather coat and wondered about Kathleen Thomas, would she have had a heart attack anyway? Cause she wouldn't. It was hardly an everyday occurrence, a bank robber with a large revolver shoots and explodes a watermelon all over you. He wondered what her daughter's name was.

The bridge looked as though it was there for eternity, each arch had a point, there were five arches so that meant ten points, they were symmetrically perfect. 'How skilled were the chaps that built it?' Reg thought to himself as he got up to walk onto the bridge. The thick cold glass clean water flowed effortlessly underneath, separating silently either side of each triangular buttress, dark green growth clinging to the larger stones wafted in an endless movement that didn't care if it was day or night, if it was hot or cold, it's only care was that the water was pure.

Flutter down but not to drown
To float and twist to be carried to the next morning mist
Two leaves, now brown, their job done,
so down and down to the one way movement
Somewhere below to take them somewhere fast and slow.

I'm going left, look its strong and sure, a little up and down but clean and pure
Are you with me my fallen leaf?
I'm for right, it's quiet and gentle and there's an eddy, I can circle.

I'm going somewhere, come with me, if you go right you'll go nowhere.
I'm going right, going nowhere but round and round
I can watch the sun, the clouds the rain
And maybe I'll hear a sound.

Goodbye Bakewell Bridge!

Reg scribbled the words in tiny writing on the back of the notelet in his cap. He considered screwing it up and dropping it into the glass water rushing underneath, to join the two leaves he'd just written about. He looked again, 'they don't even rhyme.' He thought. 'Maybe it's just the rhythm of it that makes it a poem?' He put it back into his cap. He'd go and look inside the church this afternoon and take a couple of photos of the outside. It looked like rain, one more night in Ms. Bannister's comfortable bed, a nice breakfast then he'd head south for home. He'd take a couple of large bakewell tarts back home. Rosamund would like that.

The church was like most churches, solem and quiet inside, all stained glass and oak pews with a sandstone font. Reg sat for a moment taking it all in, there was no one else around. He thought about the revolver hidden under rags in his shed. He hadn't really done a decent job of repairing the hole in the shed roof, just a piece of gritted felt glued over from the outside. He'd had to do that quickly when Rosamund was out, fortunately it soon weathered and blended in. No, he didn't need the gun anymore. He'd bury it up the top of the garden, where all the brambles were growing, then he wouldn't be tempted to play with it, touch it, look at it. He'd put it in a biscuit tin and cover it up with a rag soaked in linseed oil. He had a big bottle of that on the top shelf. When he was a boy grandad used to play cricket for Staffordshire, Reg was his first grandson and so he gave his cricket bat to him. 'I suppose', Reg thought, ' it was in the hope that he'd inherit his sporting abilities,' but he was hopeless, hand eye coordination was not the best and sporting aptitude totally missing. No, he'd probably been a disappointment to grandad.' Anyway the bat had been bound two thirds of the way down with black tape and kept almost reverently covered in a linseed oil cloth. Reg re oiled it once a year. Of course he had no one to pass it on to. That was a disappointment as well.

Bakewell was a nice town, Reg became a tourist and paid to go in 'the Old House Museum'. It was a display of ancient rural life. He wondered who had lived and who had died there. Were they happy? Who had been conceived there. Had it been plain lust or all consuming love?" who knows. Wattle and daub? He'd rather breeze block and plaster thank you! Somethings' from the past were good but most weren't. He'd try dinner in the hotel tonight.

As he walked towards the Carlton he became Leo. The angle of his cap was critical and serious in order to convey the message, along with his coat, shirt and Jeans that he was 'a person' someone you didn't mess with. He didn't have to earn respect, he silently demanded it. The engine jumped into life as though impatient to be moving. He looked at the empty lunch box beside him. It didn't fit. He reached over and placed it on the rear seat next to the two tarts. He drove South out of Bakewell on the Matlock road and thought about the notelet in his hat, should he copy it into a notebook? No, he'd just leave it where it was for now. He wondered more about David or Frank and decided it would be David first. David somehow was more comfortable with Kathleen than Frank. It was raining now.

"Hello dear, are you back?" Rosamund was playing the whole thing very low key. Reg knew that really she was worried and upset by his 'change of life'. They were settled, respectable, old, for Gods sake, what on earth was he doing?

"No, I'm a hologram controlled by Lloyds bank sent to make sure you use your credit card up to the hilt and of course not pay it all back within fifty six days."
"Were your sandwiches OK?"
"Lovely, I've brought two tarts back with me. I hope you don't mind, they can live in the back room."

Rosamund came down the stairs and looked at her husband. He was grinning with two flat cardboard boxes labeled 'The Bakewell Tart Shop.' He was smiling at her. She was glad to see him back safe and sound. She hated his new car, it was so ugly, almost vulgar. 'Whatever made him buy it?' She thought.
"Did you write your poem?"
"Yes."
"Can I see it?"
"No, it's rubbish."

"Tea?"

"Thought you'd never ask?" Reg gently kissed her on her head.

"Sausage and mash for tea tonight. Is that OK?"

"Sounds wonderful." Reg settled into the blue sofa and shot at the TV with his remote control gun. 'He'd do it tomorrow when she went shopping.' He thought. 'That is if it isn't raining.'

Chapter 8.

It wasn't rain, it was intermittent drizzle.

"Ok I'm off, Waitrose, then Marks and Sparks, then over to Gloucester for some new tennis shoes."
"OK, I'll move my car." Reg followed her out of the front door. She'd never shown any interest at all in the Carlton, from that, Reg surmised that she disliked it, even hated it. She'd never been in it. He rolled back down the drive to allow her blue beetle room to escape, after they'd waved and she'd gone he turned it on and moved up to the top of the drive. He didn't plan to go anywhere today. He clicked on the radio, Sinead O'Connor came out of the speakers singing 'Nothing Compares To You.' He sat there listening, the blown drizzle making the greenish tint of the glass more green. It made him think of their wedding day, he wore a sailor's uniform, Rosamund wore a white lacy dress. On that day nothing did compare to her. It was her day. The sun shone and everybody was happy, and so it started--------. After a few years, folk began to ask wry, veiled questions about 'the patter of tiny feet' but after a few more years they presumed it was the cat and only the cat. They'd talked many times about seeking medical help but it seemed so invasive, so personal so they didn't bother. Reg turned everything off and went back inside. He'd do it now.

There was a new large empty biscuit tin under the sink, it was from last Christmas, Rosamund was very careful about throwing things away that might come in handy one day. He loved his shed, he liked the wood, the smell, somehow it was his world, he knew where everything was. A place for everything and everything in it's place. Even the jam jars had labels on them. Opening the tin he placed the gun in it. It was a perfect fit. Made to measure, Reg chuckled to himself, he had another tin, an old oval shaped orange Birds biscuit tin for the ammunition. He wrapped it in a soft cotton rag and poured the Linseed oil all over it. The rag would gradually soak it all up. He took one last look and put the lid on. He wondered whether or not to seal the joint with tape but decided against it. He wondered if he should throw it in the river, but that was too final. It was such a beautiful thing, It was like saying goodbye to an old exciting friend, someone who always brightened up your day. Reg grabbed his spade and headed out towards the very back of the back garden, to where the big bramble bush was trying to bring down the stone wall.

Nobody could see him digging the deep hole, maybe the cat had died and he was burying it. Within half an hour it was gone, within a month it would be overgrown.

At home, he was Reg, he didn't wear a hat, he wore his usual safe coloured clothes. If he went out it would depend on his mood and destination. The corner shop for a paper, some milk, a loaf, it was Reg. Even the local town was sometimes Reg but any further, any place he was anonymous, he was Leo. Reg washed off his spade, dried it and stood it in it's place at the back of the shed. The rain was coming harder now, he'd put on a waterproof and wash down the Lotus, the rain would wash away the suds, save him from getting the hose out.

After tea Rosamund and Reg settled on the sofa for Coronation Street

"Do you think Bet and Alec could really run a pub? You know, in real life?" Rosamund asked.
"Doubt it, they're actors, not workers, it's hard graft running a pub." Reg responded.
"How would you know?"
"Grandad used to be the steward of a foundry social club, I used to go with him in the mornings. It's hard graft and late nights."
"You going off anywhere next Monday?"

It was a pointed question, disguised and hidden in mundane conversation.

"Lampeter."
"Where's Lampeter?"
"Somewhere in West Wales."
"What do you want to go there for?"
"It's the oldest University in Wales, the third oldest in the UK after Oxford and Cambridge. The name sounds so romantic, the place is just aching for my poetic skills."
"Sounds like a fish." Rosamund retorted.
"That's a Lamprey and they were a delicacy in ancient times."
"I'm glad we're not ancient then. You will be careful Reg won't you, driving all over the place in that horrible car."
"Of course, you know me, Mr. Conservative Careful."
"I don't think I do know you Reg, after thirty two years I've no idea who you are."

Reg looked at her and smiled.

"Don't be silly. Tea?"
"Yes please."

Reg got up and left the room. He popped his head back around the door.

"And there's the remains of a Norman Castle within the university campus quadrangle." Rosamund rolled her eyes.

She'd packed him a lunch box. They'd had a lovely piece of roast pork for Sunday dinner. The crackling was just perfect. Reg didn't know how she did it, whenever he'd tried to cook a pork roast the crackling was leathery, chewy and soggy. Yes the sandwiches would be cold roast pork and stuffing.

As well as the romance of the town, the road that branched right off the A 40 just after Llandovery looked interesting, quite narrow with lots of twists and bends. On the map it looked quiet, not much traffic, not many people would want to go to Lampeter on a damp Monday morning. Rosamund looked at him in his 'new man' clothes, he'd brought a new bag, an ex Royal Navy 'pussers grip' from the Army and Navy Store in Gloucester. It had M J W stencilled in black paint on both sides. She wondered who he was. She wondered who Reg was. He certainly wasn't the man who'd worked in Hereford Police station for all those years. His old brown Kodak Brownie was slung around his neck. His new cap sat at a jaunty angle on his head. He'd lost most of his hair. The whole centre of his head was bald, as though a motorbike with a big fat tyre had ridden over his head and taken all his hair, leaving just the sides and back. His cap hid it. 'He did look better with it on' she thought but still wasn't convinced about the leather jacket. He pecked her on the cheek as he opened the front door.

"See you in a few days love."
"Reg?"
"What?"
"Please be careful in that car, it looks like a racing car."
"It's a four door Vauxhall saloon Rosamund, how much more careful do you want me to be?"
"Very careful."

Reg looked at his wife as he closed the door. He walked the few steps down the drive and got into the Carlton as Leo Thrust.

"Cause I'm leaving on a jet plane,
Don't know when I'll be back again,
Oh babe, I hate to go.

So kiss me and smile for me,
Tell me that you'll wait for me,

Hold me like you'll never let me go!

Reg couldn't remember all the words of the Peter Paul and Mary song. It wasn't a jet plane. It wasn't a MIG 29 Fighter, but it was as close as you could get on a road. The acceleration when the twin turbos kicked in was phenomenal. He loved the feeling. Reg noticed that he was doing that more and more. Bursting into song when something triggered his memory. He'd have to stop. Leo wasn't a singing man. Of course you had to be careful with the accelerator in the wet, or even the damp or you'd be swapping ends pretty quickly.

"As free as the wind." Reg stopped himself singing and rummaged through the glove box to pull out another tape. ' Complete and Unbelievable - The Otis Redding Dictionary of Soul'. That would do, he remembered buying the tape in some cheap shop somewhere, he loved 'Ton of Joy'. He could never play it in the Civic, somehow it felt stifled, almost strangled, but here in the Lotus it was free to bounce around. Reg dropped it into fifth gear and sped past three struggling lorries as they clawed up the long incline. The Carlton didn't notice the gradient.

He'd save the lunch box for later, from his youth he remembered Llandovery and the eternal quandary. There was a really homely cafe that sold tea and Welsh cakes. He could eat Welsh cakes with butter forever but three doors down was an excellent little fish and chip shop. Cod and chips with lots of vinegar was very tempting. He'd have to eat them outside of course, didn't want the Lotus to smell. If he had fish and chips he probably wouldn't eat his sandwiches later so tea and Welsh cakes it was. There was a cobbled triangle of parking places in front of the cafe with plenty of spaces. Leo noticed that unconsciously he was picking parking places with plenty of room on the drivers side so that he didn't have to squeeze out of the car. That was just too tiresome.

He felt like an observer. There were no 'lone' people in the cafe except him. Mostly middle aged farming couples, hardly speaking to each other but very much couples. Nothing much had changed from his memories, still red and white check tablecloths and cream wallpaper. He ordered a large mug of tea with four Welsh cakes and listened to the musical lilting cadence of conversation. One couple were speaking in Welsh. 'Bet they voted 'Plaid Cymru' Reg thought. Most of the people in there glanced up at him as he entered and immediately classified him as English, a foreigner, most definitely not a local dressed like that.

The indicator light on the dash clicked away as he turned right off the A 40 and obeyed the signs for Lampeter. After the trees and fields had taken over from the few stone houses and buildings the road got narrower. The Lotus came alive as Leo picked lines and routes through bends and corners. He felt alive, he could feel the battle between power and adhesion, hear the source of that power, control that power with his foot. There was no room in his mind for anything else, the journey was consuming all his attention. The damp road, all his energy. He slowed to a halt, almost sweating, as he approached the town's name sign. Reaching into the glove box he felt for his Kodak. The sign was big and blue, obviously that wouldn't show as the film was black and white. It carried the name of Lampeter in English and Welsh and the fact that the town was twinned with Saint Germain Sur Moine. He knew 'sur' was 'on' so presumably 'Moine' was a river and St Germain somewhere in France. Somebody passed by in a dirty dark brown Austin Princess with a broken front left headlight and stared at him as he took the picture in the clammy drizzle. Lumpy Welsh hills surrounded the town which was just a support act for the University and a weekly market. The streets, sprinkled with small shops, their coloured facades injecting some colour into the grey brownness of the solid streets. 'What on earth could he write his poem about?' Leo thought as he cruised into town.

'This Welsh foray was just a diversion.' He admitted to himself as he drove slowly trying to take everything in. He'd come simply to conceal the fact that he had to go back to Richmond. To right a wrong. To do his best. To at least know what the repercussions of his frightening adventure were. He'd go to Richmond next week. He'd tell Rosamund he was just going north. The Royal Oak Hotel, that would do, obviously an old coaching Inn judging by the narrow tunnel-like entry. Leo eased the car slowly and carefully through it into a pleasant courtyard.

Somehow Lampeter couldn't escape it's historic fate. A university created to train clergy for the Anglican Church dominated the town. Here you just couldn't help but ponder and examine life. Maybe it was the two tumbling rivers that merged nearby, maybe it was the format of the surrounding green hills, maybe it was just because it was remote and an effort to get to. Reg wandered the little town. He could almost sense, see or hear sheep or cattle being driven through the wide streets to their market pens. Ever vigilant, ever obedient, black and white dogs with lolling tongues chivvying at the back. Behind them men dressed like the hills who had never been to London, Paris or even Birmingham but who lacked for nothing in their complete internal lives. A trail of black shit to be avoided behind, whilst quiet young academics discussed Islam in a tea shop. There was the obligatory tall stone cenotaph with a cross on top in the centre of the town. Etched names slowly disappearing with the years, wind and raindrops. Were you only real if there was somebody still alive who could remember your living self. After that what! When the icy wind has smoothed your name from the granite. Did you ever exist? If you hadn't fathered a child? If you'd never been a mother? Did it matter at all if you existed or not? Reg looked at his reflection in the large glass window of a small closed haberdashery shop and wondered if he mattered at all. He had no one to leave his legitimate wealth to. No son to inherit his fast car, no daughter to give his house to. A twenty five year mortgage seemed like unreachable eternity when they'd bought the house. In a flash it had gone. A soup of cream and grey office spiced with the vivid colour of Southern France every summer and the smell of local wine 'caves' in afternoon sleepy sun had made it compress into a minute of life. Now what!

'The Taliesin Tea Rooms' It was painted in orange script onto a dark blue headboard that ran the whole length above the front window. The bell clanged above the door of the tea shop. There was always a bell.
A Celtic dark haired forty something waitress come cashier come cleaner come cook asked what he wanted whilst looking at him. Reg pushed the ashtray away to the furthest edge of the table.

"Tea and Welsh Cakes please." She wrote it down on a little pad. "Lots of butter please."
She smiled.
"Not worrying about your weight then?"
"I worry all the time, but occasionally I fail."
"Not many men admit to failing." The conversation immediately deepened as though the tea shop was a dark secluded room deep in the bowels of the ancient University.
"I'm not a man. I'm still a boy, bit like Peter Pan."
"I can see that. Do you have any wings underneath that leather jacket?"
"No, I left them at the Royal Oak."
"Why are you here?" It was a personal intrusive question that Reg's smile and friendliness had permitted her to ask. She had high cheekbones that made her look pretty but a receding chin line that didn't.
"Write a poem."
"What about?"
"No idea yet?"
"Will you show it to me before you leave?"
"Would I get an extra free Welsh Cake if I did?"
She looked into his eyes.
"Yes. With lots of butter." She laughed.
"Then I will." She turned away to get his tea and cakes.
"Are you a mother?"
"Yes, two girls."
"Then I'll write about you." She blushed. "What's 'Taliesin'?"
"He was a sixth century Welsh poet, The chief Bard to the king's court."
"Not sure if I can compete with him."

"Just try your best." She touched his arm as she put down a small plate of five Welsh Cakes.

Reg pondered if it made a difference if he wrote his poem outside in the cold or inside in the warm. He decided it would have to be outside. Poetry always seemed to be written from a position of angst, hard to be creative if you're comfortable. He'd write it somewhere near the Norman Keep if he could identify it.

"Which bit of it is the Norman Keep?" Reg asked a youth thin, tall, ginger haired student. "What's a Norman Keep?" He had blank light blue eyes that went with his very white skin and his very ginger hair. "There's one of our tutors over there, probably get a sensible answer from him. I'm pretty new here."
"Thank you." Said Reg as he moved towards the briskly walking man in a black gown but no hat.
"Excuse me Sir, could you tell me which bit of the quadrangle is the old Norman Keep?" The man's age and dress warranted a respectful 'Sir'.

The man stopped and looked Reg up and down, taking a while to decide that his slightly extrovert dress matched his knowledgeable question.

"It's just that corner over there, if you look closely the colour of the stone changes where the join is."
"So it does, thank you." The tutor carried on his journey, almost marching.

On the corner by the dark stone, just on the grass was a wooden bench. There had been a plaque on it, he could tell by the light imprint but it had gone. 'Probably donated by the family of a famous principal or master' thought Reg as he sat. He took out his notelet pad and biro. He decided he'd only allow himself five minutes, it had to be spontaneous and raw, nothing contrived.

Don't sit there, sit elsewhere!
My job is to stare and stare and stare.

Your just an old stone, albeit cut shaped and placed,
Whilst I am a bench, sit down and rest I say.

I am old but still good, I've seen many starry nights.
You are young but made of wood, not very good,
The sun, rain and stars will destroy you!

Who are you? Who are you to say?
I'm here day after day, after day.
People like me, I support them, give them time together, time to relax while children play.

Your day is my year, you'll not last many I fear!

But once I was alive, you were only dust.

I'm now stone hard, nothing can touch me, I won't rust.

I had a mother sit on me today,
She was a mother of two
She didn't notice you!

Reg chuckled at his attempt, it was rubbish, still it might get him an extra Welsh Cake tomorrow.

His room at The Royal Oak was - well - just a hotel room. Comfortable, warm, dry but exhausted by feet and souls that constantly passed through but never stayed. No one wanted to stay, to make it theirs. It was always hello and goodbye, never a home.

It was tonight, as every night, not the MIG. Not the blackness of space. Not the curve and blueness of earth. It was a life gone, maybe a family destroyed, blown apart just like the watermelon. He was glad he'd buried the gun, it was irresistible, it controlled him, he didn't control it. He copied his poem onto a sheet of hotel notepaper then turned out the light.

She lowered her eyes to look at him.

"Have you got it?" She asked. Her voice a Welsh melody.
"Yes." Reg pulled out the paper from the heavy flapped breast pocket of the leather jacket and passed it to her. She stood at the table and read it.
"Can I keep it?" She asked.
"Of course, it's for you."
She looked at him before folding it back up and slipping it into her skirt pocket. She turned away to get his order.

A mug of tea and six Welshcakes with lots of butter were delivered silently.

Somehow the journey back didn't seem so much fun, the road was dry but he just didn't feel exuberante, he popped a Carpenter's cassette in.

"And every road that takes me,
Takes me down."

It was definitely suicide music. It made him think of the little round red plastic solitaire set with white pegs he had as a boy. How excited he used to get when he managed to do it. It made him think of the hole in his shed roof.

What's it all about, Alfie?
Is it just for the moment we live?

Cilla Black was almost as depressing as Karen Carpenter. Reg floored the accelerator, the big car chirped with glee and shot forward towards the next bend.

Chapter 9.

Terry Dixon knocked politely on the open door of Ken France's office and went in. Ken was wrestling with Irish 'knockers' and antique auction 'ringing'. He was convinced they were connected but didn't know how. Ken was stick thin with dark hair, his mean disposition hid a heart of gold.

"Letter for you boss." Terry placed a grubby white envelope on the desk.

Ken glanced at the smudged spidery biro writing on the envelope.

'Detective Inspector Ken France - private.'

"Who's it from?"
"One Hubert Edward Carr - deceased." Ken tried successfully to disguise his shock.
"When did that happen?"
"Yesterday morning."
"Where?"
"Hospital wing of Strangeways, pancreatic cancer apparently, very quick, a matter of weeks."
"OK Terry, leave it there and close the door on the way out."
"Yes Boss." It was unusual for Ken to have his door closed. 'Surely a career tow-rag like Carr dying wouldn't be of any significance. Waste of time, waste of taxpayers money, good riddance. Ten years for the Yorkshire Building Society job was getting away with it lightly as far as he was concerned, especially as there was a firearm involved.

Hubert Edward Carr and Kenneth James France had gone through primary school together. Hubby Carr always beat him at conkers and running but Ken had passed the 'eleven plus' and went to Huddersfield Grammar School, Hubby hadn't and went to the comp. Ken had arrested him many times when he was a young PC but he always got a cup of tea at his mum's whenever he called 'on enquiries'.

He looked at the letter for a while before opening it.

The letter inside was just as scruffy and grubby as the envelope.

Ken,
If you're reading this, I ain't around no more. That'll be a big relief to your blokes!

Anyway, I know you and I have had our ups and downs, gone our separate ways, taken different paths and all that but we both know that deep down we quite liked each other. I've done lots of bad things all my life but always stopped short of hurting people, you know that, so please, just this once, believe me when I tell you that I didn't do the Building Society job in Richmond. I'm gone now but there's somebody running around out there who did do it. I've no idea who did, it wasn't a 'local' job or I would know. It's over to you now Ken.

Hubby.

PS, three days soaking in vinegar then a week up the chimney makes your conker indestructible.

Ken put the letter back into the envelope and placed it in the top drawer of his desk. He pushed back his chair, stretched out his feet and put his hands behind his head. Christine, one of the typists knocked and came straight in. She was surprised to see him obviously contemplating 'something'.

"Christine, get me a coffee will you love? And find out where and when Hubby Carr's funeral will be." It was unusual for Ken to call her love. He seemed to be in a funny mood. "Oh and get D.S. O'Keefe to come and see me when he gets back in."

Rick O'Keefe was the smartest on his team. An affable, quiet, round faced Irishman who everybody liked but who was sharp as a razor. He'd verbally back you into a corner from which there was no escape other than a guilty admission.

"Rick, thanks for coming, shut the door will you? Then take a seat. Do you remember that Building Society job a couple of years ago at Richmond?"
"Of course. Hubby Carr went down for it."
"Well Hubby's just died of cancer and I've reason to believe it wasn't him. I want you to reopen the case, treat it as a cold case. There's been considerable advancement in DNA profiling these last few years. Have a look will you? I feel we at least owe it to Hubby to get the right offender."
Rick looked quizzically at his boss.
"To be fair boss Carr was a career criminal, never did a legit day's work in his life. Bloody good thing getting him ten years, plus we got a detected crime out of it."
"He was my friend at school, he didn't do it Rick, find out who did."
"Yes Boss."

Chapter 10.

"Is that you love?"

Rosamund shouted through from the kitchen as she heard a key enter the front door lock and the door open.

"No, it's a Mongolian Death Worm. I'm so poisonous that just to touch me means instant death. How about a kiss?"

"I'll risk it." She came through into the hall smiling whilst drying her hands on a tea towel.

"No designer stubble today?"

"No Pierre Cardin told me that if it got itchy it was OK to have a shave." She took his bag.

"Go and sit down and I'll get you a cuppa. Beans and poached eggs on toast for tea. Is that OK?"

"What! No Welshcakes? My other serving wench gave me six Welshcakes with lots of butter. She wanted me to marry her but I said no, I wouldn't have been able to cope with two teenage daughters living in the bathroom.

"I'm not Welsh Reg, you'll have to marry your Welsh 'tart' for that."

"No! No! The tart was Bakewell, Bakewell tarts, Welshcakes are flat round things."

"Sit down, here's your tea. Did she have large breasts?"

"No, she had two teenage daughters."

Rosamund could sense the joking conversation was straying into uncomfortable territory.

"What was your poem about?"

"An ancient stone in a wall and an old wooden bench."

"Ummm, sounds fascinating, are you going to put them in a book?"

"No, in my hat."

Reg turned on the TV. Rosamund went back into the kitchen. She wasn't coping at all well with his strange retired lifestyle. Rosamund emptied his bag in front of the washing machine. Nothing! Not a clue as to what he'd really been up to, just dirty socks and underwear and one shirt, a small polythene bag with his toothbrush and razor. Either he was doing nothing or he was very careful. God! She wished he'd just un-retire and go back to work!

"Thinking of buying a canal boat for the holidays Rosamund, I'm bored with France. What do you think?"

She pretended not to hear and went back into the kitchen to butter his toast.

Reg liked his Sunday TV, 'Songs of Praise', Antiques Roadshow, and 'Last of The Summer Wine', were his favourites. He hadn't mentioned the canal boat again so perhaps it was just a bit of a dream. They couldn't afford one anyway. Not after he'd spent all that money on the awful car. She had to ask.

"So where is it this week?"

"No idea, up North, I prefer the North to the South, somehow it feels more - ." There was a pause as he took a sip of tea and thought. "More tangible, More gritty, somehow more real."

"I'm not sure what's real any more Reg. Why can't you just be normal like everybody else? You know, grow veg in the back garden, buy the paper everyday in the shop and moan about the weather."

Reg looked at her.

"I've been normal, dull, boring, reliable all my life Rosamund. I'm up to here with it."

"But I like it Reg. What about me?"

"What's actually changed for you Rosamund? Other than I'm away for a couple of nights a week. I'll probably get bored with that soon and then I'll probably take up collecting sticks of rock." He stretched out his arm, smiled and squoze her leg.

"What were her daughters' names?"

Reg nearly choked on his tea.

"For goodness sake Rosamund, I've no idea I was just making polite conversation to a waitress in a cafe."

"We should have tried to adopt Reg."

"Yes, we should have, but it's too late now. What are we eating?"

"Lamb chops, new potatoes, runner beans and carrots, mint sauce and gravy."

"My absolute favourite. I love you Rosamund Moorcroft."

"No you don't. If you did, you'd behave yourself."

Reg settled back to watch 'Compo'.

"Doug next door has got himself some chickens. I hope he doesn't get a cockerel. It's a fallacy you know, they crow all night, not just at dawn."

"Shall we eat in the dining room or have it on our knees?" Reg smirked at his disgusting thoughts. Rosamund knew what he was thinking and scowled at him.

"In here if you don't mind love." Reg laughed as Compo flew out of his wellies and over the stone wall.

Monday mornings were beginning to become stressful. She didn't like him going but didn't say and dutifully packed him a lunch box. There were two cold beef and horseradish sauce sandwiches. She slipped the note between them.

Think of me when you're eating these,
Think of us before you drive fast
Cause I don't want this lunch to be your last!
I love you Reg Moorcroft, come home safe to me.

At the side of the sandwiches were two small Mandarin oranges and two Welsh Cakes.

The new Reg Moorcroft said goodbye, kissed her tenderly and left holding his 'Pussers Grip' and his orange lunch box. A few steps down the drive he stopped and turned.

"I'm sure he's got a cockerel, did you hear it at about three thirty this morning?"
"No."

Leo Thrust turned the key then drove sedately and carefully away. He knew she'd be watching from the bedroom window. All roads led North. He rummaged in the glove box. 'Best of Matt Munro'. No, that was Reg, Reg liked it a lot, as did his mother, she also liked Engelbert Humperdink and Max Bygraves, which he didn't. David Bowie, Ziggy Stardust, that was far more leo. The first track burst into the car.

'Time takes a cigarette and puts it in your mouth
You pull on a finger,
Then another finger,
Then cigarette

--You're a Rock and Roll Suicide!'

It took him back to his shed, he should really conceal the hole from the inside, just in case. It wasn't leaking so he'd get round to it one day. He wondered if his perfect gun was still perfect, hidden away in its grave.

The junction of the M5 and M6 was always busy, especially this time of the morning. High speed on a twisty A road was the preferred environment for the Lotus. Inching along in a traffic jam operating the absurdly heavy clutch was hell. The car wasn't happy at all, neither was Leo. He considered eating one of his sandwiches out of sheer boredom but decided against it.

Whenever the motorway was clear the big car took a deep breath like the loosening of the reins on a lean racehorse, desperate to lengthen it's stride and gallop. The plan was a circular loop, up the M6 to Kendal, across the Yorkshire Dales on the A684, then a slight left diversion up to Richmond. After that back south on the M1. But first it was a dive left to Blackpool for the night. In his cap were two poems and two addresses, all on sticky yellow notelets. He'd drive to Blackpool, and park somewhere where he could see the sea and the tower then eat his lunch. After Ziggy Stardust had played for a second time Leo put Matt Munro in the slot.

'Born Free, as free as the wind blows,
As free as the grass grows,
Born free to follow your heart.'

Leo chuckled to himself, his heart had very nearly been in outer space, not many people could say that. He took the slip road West off the M6. Apparently on a clear day you could see the Blackpool Tower from the M6 but today was cloudy.

The sign was square, white with black writing and read - Welcome to Blackpool - Twin Town - Bottrop Germany. - Please Drive Carefully. Leo stopped the car, put the Hazards on then got out with his Brownie. He looked at the little window, eight more frames to go.
He'd only ever been to Blackpool once before with Mom and Dad, on a train to see the illuminations. He remembered that it was a clear dark cold night so it must have been in the autumn or late in the year. He seemed to remember that it had been a trip organised by dad's works.

At eleven o'clock, on a not very nice Monday morning the car park at the southern end of the promenade was virtually empty. Reg parked up facing the brown grey cold looking sea. To his right, clearly visible and not too far away was the red spire of the tower, a copy of Mr. Eiffels in Paris, half as tall and somehow not so elegant. Nevertheless it had stood the test of time and the elements that constantly made it move and sway.

He looked out to sea and opened his lunch box. He could see three people on the beach, one middle aged couple with a dog and a lone youngish man, 'probably having problems with a wife or girlfriend and doesn't notice that it's cold and damp,' Reg thought. Taking the top sandwich he saw it.

'Think of me when you're eating these,
Think of us before you drive fast
Cause I don't want this lunch to be your last!
I love you Reg Moorcroft, come home safe to me.'

Leo read it twice. 'That's a lot better than my poems.' He thought, biting into the sandwich. 'Two Welshcakes; women are so dangerously intuitive.' He did love her,he'd never loved anyone else, never even considered life without her, never seriously considered or even looked at anyone else. 'Reg Moorcroft was a model husband.' Leo thought.

Leo locked the car and looked around for a B&B. He'd never stopped in a B&B before, they always seemed like the stuff of semi-rude, almost pornographic postcards. A Norah Batty type landlady looking down the steps to a just married couple. The young wife with huge breasts that were barely able to remain in a tight short top and a young man with a huge grin on his face as she shouts 'Standing Room only tonight I'm afraid.'

'Sea View. B&B' Well it was original,' Reg thought. There was a little wooden sign dangling on two short chains. 'Vacances'. Reg pressed the highly polished bell.

It wasn't Norah Batty but it was a woman in her fifties wearing curlers and slippers.

"Excuse my appearance, going out tonight and wasn't really expecting any customers. Do come in." She had the sweetest soft brown voice.
"Do you have a room?'
"Yes! Yes! Come in, there's a cold wind." She closed the door on what was left of a grey chilly morning.
"How many nights?"
"Just the one."
"Work?"
"No. I'm a poet, want to write something about Blackpool."
She looked him up and down.
"Yes, you look like a poet, never had a famous poet stay in my place before."
"I'm not famous."
She looked at him again.
"Then why do you do it?"
"It makes me happy. What makes you happy Mrs.--------------?"

"Smith, a gin and tonic, a good man and a decent night's sleep."

"There's no such thing."

"What?"

"There's no such thing as a good man. We've all got terrible secrets."

She looked at him and laughed.

"You know, you may just be right. Room number three at the top of the stairs, cash or card?"

"Cash, how much?"

"Eight pounds fifty or a straight ten pounds if you want dinner tonight."

"Is it any good?"

"The best." She smiled. She had a nice smile, it totally changed the shape of her face, it revealed a kind, funny person who'd maybe been hurt a few times.

"A tenner it is then." Reg peeled off a note from the roll in his jacket pocket.

"Nice jacket." She said, taking the note from his hand.

"It's a Belstaff."

"Is that good?" She asked.

"Yes ----- if you have a motorbike."

"Have you got a motorbike?"

"No a car."

"I was just thinking; no sign of a helmet."

She offered the keys and Reg took them. Leo would have winked but Reg didn't.

The room and bed were like every other room and bed. He lay on it wondering if you spent your life wandering about in B&B's, cheapish hotels and the like, would that work out cheaper than a conventional house, mortgage or rent, electricity, water, the rates, telephone, insurance, general repairs and maintenance. He concluded it would be a lot cheaper but of course you wouldn't be able to have a shed. Sleep was unavoidable.

"How long does it take to walk to the tower from here Mrs Smith? Reg asked.

"About twenty minutes. Depending on how fast you walk."

"These days the only time I walk fast is when I need to go to the toilet, then all your aches and pains suddenly disappear. But you wouldn't know as you're too young."

"We women suffer as well you know." She looked directly at him.

"Kids?"

"Two, a boy and a girl."

"Husband?"

"Gone, a younger model."

"Oh." Reg didn't have to say anymore, the understanding and sympathy were written on his face and in his eyes.

"What time for dinner?"

"Anytime after six."

"What is it?"

"Lamb chops, new potatoes, peas, carrots, gravy and mint sauce."

"Any runner beans?"

She stopped and once again looked at him.

"I'll do you some."

"Thank you." Reg headed for the white front door then turned.

"Thank you."

'On a clear day
Rise and look around you
And you'll see who you are
On a clear day,
How it will astound you
That the glow of your being outshines every star.'

It was from a musical but he couldn't remember which one, he knew the tune though. The words made him laugh. Rosamund had said that she didn't know who he was anymore. If he was honest neither did he. Torn between Reg and Leo he looked out at the vista of Lancashire then the other way to the dull power of the Irish Sea. There was no one else on the viewing platform, three hundred and eighty feet up on a cold grey day wasn't a popular place to be. It wasn't a clear day.

The tower sat safely on a pile of red brick. It was a place of hope, aspiration and excitement but only for the young. Years made you cynical.

Will she be there tonight?
Will he like my dress?
Will she think about me tonight?
What about my hair? It's a mess.

What should I take? Some flowers? Some chocolates?
Maybe a Cadbury's Flake?
What if he tries to kiss me?
I'm sure I'll feint. I can't eat, I can't wait.

Get out of the bathroom,
You've been there for hours.
Sorry Dad, just taking a shower.

You're not going out wearing that,
Dad, it's the latest fashion, I'll wear a hat.

Will you take me in the car?
No, get the bus, it's not that far.
But it's raining my hair will frizz
Dad I'm getting all of a tizz.

Be calm my beautiful girl
Your dad is here to take you to the ball,
I hope he'll love you as much as me,
Maybe he should come home for tea.

You're the best dad in the world!

Reg stuffed the notelet in his hat and pulled it down.

She was right, the dinner was good, the mint sauce was homemade, the new potatoes perfect, probably Pembrokeshires. She hadn't mentioned the pudding, apple crumble and custard. Mrs Smith certainly could cook. Mr. Smith was a fool.

Breakfast was traditional. Reg felt he wouldn't need to eat again until tonight. Mrs Smith smiled sincerely as he left, giving him a card should ever be in Blackpool again. Leo slipped into the driver's seat and slipped in Karen Carpenter who immediately slipped out with 'Masquerade'.

'We tried to talk it over but the words got in the way.'

He turned it off as he threaded his way east out of the seaside town and pointed the powerful car towards Kendal, the moors and Richmond.

God the moors were bleak, it got colder, wetter and bleaker as he ascended. Sedbergh Bainbridge, and Leyburn came and went. He was crossing from the White Rose of Lancashire to the Red Rose of Yorkshire. From times when the crown of England was settled in these drizzly hard cold parts and not the balm of London to now, when his fast chariot with it's hidden horses covered the sixty miles effortlessly and quickly.

A left turn out of Leyburn, twenty five more minutes then there it was, affixed to a grey stone pillar for all eternity, immovable, as robust as Mount Everest. Three black and white plates. 'Richmond' topped by a red heraldic crest. 'Twinned with Nord - Fron Kommune (Norway), at the right side was a small black shield with a prancing white horse. Twinned with St. Aubin Du Cormier (France).

It took him back to his last visit, the train, the watermelon, the gun, the fear, the excitement. He wondered if you could really be excited without fear. Was that the ultimate height of excitement? His Brownie clicked. An old man driving an old Citroen DS stared at him as he stood in the rain with his camera. Reg thought it very apt that the car was French. He didn't think Norway made any cars.

Before turning the key Leo took off his cap and took out the notelet with the two addresses on. It was two in the afternoon, he decided to find a hotel, think about things then see what tomorrow would bring. There was no carefully packed lunch box today. He was hungry but that was good. Leo should be lean and mean. There was no plan.

The Black Lion looked good but the parking looked difficult so it was The Kings Head. Leo stayed in the car but Reg got out. His first visit had been a blur, he'd noticed nothing, all he remembered was nearly being knocked over by a van as he crossed the road towards the Building Society, being shouted at by the driver and then the 'event'. Once the gun was in his hand he changed, bit like the 'Incredible Hulk' getting angry but in Reg's case he didn't turn green he became Leo. An invincible ego, super confident, scared of nothing, authority poured out of him delivered by his voice. Compliance was demanded and given.

The little town looked beautiful in the fickle afternoon. The park, the castle with it's Norman Keep dominating the clustering subjects that fawned at it's feet. At two o'clock it was fish and chips in a newspaper on a bench. 'Rosamund would never do this', he thought. 'Far too bohemian'. He made sure he went nowhere near the Yorkshire Building Society Office. It was unavoidable in the market square, he tried not to glance at it. The strange 'obelisk' towered from the centre of the square. The square tower of the nearby Holy Trinity Church, beckoning and persuading people to come in through it's open doors. It made Reg think of a needle and thimble, The cobbles made all the traders' stalls uneven and somehow more higgledy-piggledy than they actually were. The cheese stall slanted a bit one way, whilst the hat stall next to it slanted the other way, the bits of grass growing tenaciously between the cobbles somehow added to the market kaleidoscope. The chips were delicious, the batter on the cod still crisp despite lots of vinegar. People mooched and looked or moved and bought depending on their urgency. Reg studied the pamphlet from the hotel as the last chips disappeared. The Culloden Tower 1746, now that looked interesting 'built to commemorate the defeat of the 'Young Pretender' Bonnie Prince Charlie'.

Oh Yes! I'm the great Pretender,
Pretending that I'm doing well,
My need is such!
I pretend too much,
I'm lonely, but no one can tell

Reg chuckled at his own thoughts. 'Fancy having the funds to build a tower to remember a defeat, you could understand a victory but a defeat? I suppose if you supported the other side, a defeat was a victory'. He thought. According to the pamphlet there was a garden that was nearer. That would do.

Richmondshire my dear,
Don't prick your finger in the market square,
Use the thimble to pray a prayer,
Pray Norman will keep his keep,
So we can lie in peaceful sleep,

The swirling Swale so washed and clean,
Falls swiftly in flood but is summer serene,
Picnics and ducks, sandwiches and children
The clean green grass, so sweet to sit on.

The market square, as big as you get,
If you can't buy it here then you don't need it yet,
People walk by, some plod, some skip
But most just trudge, no smile on their lips,

And here I am, a voyeur, a stranger,
Much better than being a visiting danger,
I can take time to look and know
Then disappear before the winter snow.

He'd have a look round the market and the garden then have a little nap in his hotel room before eating tonight. 'The hotel, a restaurant? He didn't know, just go with the flow.' For gods sake stop it, everything you think doesn't have to rhyme! He thought to himself.

Dinner was steak and kidney pie, mash, carrots and broccoli, followed by Rhubarb and Greek style thick yogurt. It made him sleepy so he went to bed early. Before sleeping he took out the notelet and looked at the addresses. Which one? David Alwin Thomas, 16 Frances Road. He felt sure she'd have married a David. Anyway 'Quakers Lane' who'd want an address like that?

Reg got up early, had a quick breakfast in the hotel, in fact he was the first in the hotel dining room then headed out to his car. The breakfast had been good but he'd barely noticed it, his thoughts elsewhere, his focus on Frances Street. He'd walked by the house last night when it was dark. It was just a normal white painted rendered semi, three bedrooms he guessed. A small porch sheltered the front door and across the road was a green field. He couldn't work out if it was a park come playing field or just a field. Cars parked all the way down the road on the field side leaving the house side free with most houses having a car parked on the small front drive. It was an OK morning, dry not raining but still a bit chilly. Reg parked the Lotus about thirty yards down from the house in a vacant slot. He had a good view of the front door of number sixteen, even if you came out of a back or side door you'd still have to come out of the front drive. There was no car on the drive. He turned on the radio then turned down Dereck Jameson. When no one was within sight he just stared at number sixteen. When anyone came along he pretended to read the Daily Mirror. Not that there was much to read in 'The Mirror', he'd just grabbed it from the table in the hotel foyer. It was yesterday's paper but 'Andy Capp and Flo' was funny. It was ten to seven when he'd parked up, now it was seven thirty and nothing had happened. He was beginning to feel conspicuous even if he wasn't.

At ten to eight the front door opened. He could see a man, he stopped for a second, presumably to say goodbye to someone in the house, then walked away towards Reg.

"Shit, he wasn't in a car. Reg had got it into his head that her husband would drive to work, but this man, - if it was her husband, - was walking, and more importantly walking straight towards him. Reg buried himself in the engrossing edition of 'The Mirror'. The man didn't even glance as he walked by the car. 'Why would he.' Reg thought as he relaxed. The man was about six foot tall and thin, there was something uneasy about the way he walked, as though it wasn't autonomous, he had to put effort into it. He had dark black creased trousers and shiny clean black Doc Martin Shoes. 'Ubiquitous in the Police Service.' Reg thought. He had a kind round face with a moustache with a good head of dark wavy hair. He gave him fifty yards then got out of his car as quickly as he could. At that moment he wanted to be Reg Moorcroft in his pullover and car coat but he wasn't. He was Leo Thrust in a dark blue lumberjack shirt, tight blue jeans and a brown leather jacket. Reg had never actually followed anyone before, it was quite difficult. David walked quite fast as though he was fit, or used to walking a lot despite his awkward gait. Reg had to lengthen his stride to maintain the distance. The man, David, if it was him, was carrying an orange Tupperware lunch box, exactly like the one on the back seat. Reg muttered 'I don't believe it', to himself. The man turned left on L'Anson Road, then, after about three hundred yards the road did a ninety degree right.

Reg couldn't believe it for a second time as the man walked straight into the front door of North Yorkshire Richmond Police Station, opposite which were several marked vehicles languishing in front of garages. 'Surely not.' Thought Reg. 'Surely he's not a 'Bobby'?'

Reg carried on walking, taking a clockwise route around the rather large block up a road called Galloway Road. 'Hope that's not an omen.' Reg thought. He got back in the car and Leo drove it into L'Anson Road. Parking up within sight of the Police Station the 'Mirror' once again became fascinating reading. He didn't have to wait long, after about fifteen minutes, 'David', if it was David, came out. A traffic Warden.

'Must be working an eight four shift.' Reg started up and headed for the centre of town, the obelisk, the church, the Yorkshire Building Society Office. The latter to be avoided at all costs. He'd spend the day as a tourist, visit the Culloden Tower, and the Green Howards Regimental museum which ironically was in the Holy Trinity Church in the square. He could never quite reconcile the military with religion. One was a body of trained and equipped men whose purpose was to kill other people. You could dress it in whatever clothes you wanted to, defense of the realm, maintenance of peace and order, protection of freedom and human rights but at the end of the day a gun is used to kill people. Then the clergy, reverends, vicars, call them what you will seemed to tag along as a balm for their actions, to make it OK to kill a man because you were right, you had God on your side, you must have as there's a holy man dressed in white, somewhere behind you. No, it was a strange relationship. Interesting though, sixteen Victoria crosses and three George crosses. He wondered if the recipients were really extraordinarily brave or had just accepted that they were going to die anyway so might as well get it over with and just charged whatever or wherever then were really surprised to find they were still alive, or correct in the first place and not able to be surprised. It filled a gap before lunch.

Lunch was ham, egg and chips in a small cafe in a small street. Sometimes the simple things are the best. At the table over a cup of tea he read today's Telegraph, it had more words in it than the Mirror, then it was a stroll back to his car. He was thankful to see that there was no ticket on the windscreen. Reg chuckled at the irony of his thoughts. A quick nap in the hotel then he'd park up in sight of the Police Station about ten to four.

It started to drizzle as he went to his car, summer in the north was just winter without snow and ice but somehow he could feel the attraction of the place. Everything happens despite something. The stone of the buildings somehow rebuffed everything the world could throw at it.

There he was, ten past four, heading away from home. Where was he going? He seemed more relaxed now, as though his day's work was over and the stress had left his body. His walking was easier and slower. Reg slotted in about fifty yards behind with an umbrella and the Telegraph. Where was he going?

The Ship Inn should have been a house. Sandwiched between two conventional stone terraced houses it was rendered and painted white. The ground in front of it fell away as it gently descended to the River Swale half a mile away. It's doors were open and the off duty traffic warden went in. Reg walked past the pub and on down Frenchgate just to waste time before turning around.

It had that unavoidable smell that all pubs had, a mixture of smoke, detergent, sometimes Dettol, whiffs of toilets, and alcoholic drinks. No matter what the cleaning regime was, there was always 'that smell'.

It was early, four forty five. David, if that was who he was, was the only other customer. He was sitting in the corner by the window in front of a small square table reading a local paper with what looked like a pint of shandy in front of him. He wore a greenish waterproof which could have been a 'Barbour' but there was no little enamel badge on the lapel so he thought it might be a cheaper copy. The man took it off and placed it on the chair beside him. He had a long sleeved light grey knitted jumper over his blue uniform shirt. He'd removed what was probably a black clip tie and the neck of his shirt was open. He nodded to Reg as he came in.

"Yes? What can I get you?" The bartender was a man in his forties with a black beard and a developing beer gut. Reg surveyed the pumps.
"Pint of Newcastle Brown please."
"Never seen you in here before." he said as he grasped and pulled the pump handle.
"That's because I've never been in here before." Reg proffered a pound note to the man.
"Need another twenty pence unfortunately." The man clicked a sound as his head tilted to one side. Reg fumbled in the tight right hand pocket of his jeans for a twenty pence piece.

"There you go, nothing's cheap these days is it?" Reg had half turned away from the bar so that his comment could be picked up by the Barman or 'David'. David glanced up and smiled.

"They even charge you for a glass of tap water in this pub. It's the landlord, he was born mean. Weren't you Collin?"

Colin glowered.

"A man's got to make a living. I'm not a bloody charity, though some might think so spending half his days lounging in the comfort of my heated room."

"It's a 'Public House' and I'm a member of the Public, just the same as errrm---------.'

"Reg."

"Just the same as Reg here. Come and join me Reg, usually there's not a soul comes into this place til after six, be good to talk to a fresh face."

"Well I don't think my face has ever been described as 'fresh' before ---------."

"David, David Thomas, how do you do?"

Reg put his pint down on the table and shook the offered hand. It was warm and sincere. It made Reg feel ashamed of past events.

"So where are you from?"

"The Midlands, just the English side of Wales."

"What brings you up here?"

Reg took a long draught of the beer as he weighed up which lie was more plausible.

"I've just retired so I've decided to visit places I've never been to before, take a picture and write a poem."

David looked him up and down.

"Yes I can see a bit of a poet in you."

"You're right, it is a bloody bit as well, they're rubbish."

They both laughed.

"I take it you're a Police Officer." Reg said.

David looked at him again.

"Why do you say that?"

"Blue shirt, black trousers pressed and creased, clean shiny Doc Martin shoes."

"Actually I'm a Traffic Warden, even more unpopular than Police Officers so I have to be careful who I admit that to."

"I'm a retired Crime Analyst, worked in Hereford Police Station for nearly twenty years."

"That explains it then."

"Do you want another pint?" Reg asked.

"Love one but it's only a shandy. Where are you staying?"

"The King's Head, it's OK, nothing special."

"How long are you here for?"

"Two nights then my wife says I have to come back home."

"Any kids?"

"No, just a cat. You?"

"A daughter, Aveena, she's seventeen."

Collin brought the drinks over and put them on the table.

"Bet you and your wife are as proud as punch of her."

"I am, but Kathleen, her mum died a short while ago, heart attack then a coma from which she never recovered."

"Oh, sorry to hear that." David had no idea how sorry the man sitting next to him really was. Reg was almost flattened by the confirmation that this was indeed the family he'd destroyed. "How did your daughter take that?"

"Badly at first but she's a tough bright girl, she's sought of taken on the role of my carer, she does the shopping but my sister Vanessa comes in and cooks for us. I'm trying to persuade her to do a bit of cleaning, offered to pay her but she won't hear of it."

"And you? What about you?"

David looked into Reg's eyes then turned towards his pint.

"I'll never get over it, I talk to her all the time, we were inseparable for twenty five years. I'm not sure I can do my job much longer, some bloke or woman screaming their head off at me for a ten quid ticket just doesn't register on my 'bad things' scale. Funny innit?"

"What?"

"How you can open up to a total stranger about deep personal issues."

"It's because they are strangers and will probably remain so and have no effect on your life. Share a bag of crisps?"

"Yes OK, Collin will think it's Christmas all this money flowing into his till."

"Your daughter going onto university?" Reg asked.

"No, She'd love to, the house is full of animals. At the last count there were two rabbits, three hamsters, two guinea pigs, some mice and a rat. It smells a bit, she wants to be a mammalogist, a vet, but the money's a problem. Kathleen's funeral just about wiped out my savings, a degree and then five years training as a vet is financially in cloud cuckoo land. She says she's going to work in Marks and Spencers. She's only doing that for me."

David Thomas was almost in tears. Reg made an excuse.

"Sorry David got to go, make a phone call to my wife, report in, you know how it is."

David cheered up into a false smile.

"Yes! Yes! Very nice to meet you Reg."

Reg held out his hand.

"Same time, same place tomorrow?" Reg cocked his head to one side in a question mark, wondering if he was pushing things too far.

"Yes, that would be nice, I'll buy the crisps."

Reg smiled and left.

Walking was good for thinking. He could just push an envelope full of cash through the door in the dead of night with a note, without a note, he'd have to think about that. The beer had made him hungry. He didn't feel like going into a restaurant on his own so he'd see what was on offer at the hotel. He wondered what Aveena looked like. What a lovely name for a daughter. 'I bet it was her mother who gave her that.' Reg thought.

The evening and night were full of thoughts, so much so that the excellent meal and comfortable room were just accessories. Reg decided upon caution. He'd have a couple of pints with David tomorrow, see how that went, then go home and think about things, he hadn't got much cash with him anyway. The default position would be just to push an anonymous envelope through the letterbox.

Richmond, Richmondshire, North Yorkshire was a quiet conservative place so sleep came easily. Before it came, he wondered how he'd cope without Rosamund? He'd never considered it before. He was an only child from a working class family where hugs, kisses and 'I love yous' just didn't happen after the age of about four. It made him self-reliant and the fact that they'd never had any children had just perpetuated that reliance. He looked after Rosamund, she looked after him but if ever that changed he'd just do whatever was necessary and carry on smiling at the world. It wasn't that he didn't care. It was just the way things were. Maybe Rosamund would be relieved if he wasn't there. Sleep came.

Poached eggs and kippers with a pot of tea and some nice toast. It was a good start to the day. He thought about the difference between the subtly smoked Haddock of the 'smokies' and the strong flavour of the Herrings. He thought that today he'd do the Culloden Tower and the Richmondshire Museum. Then his thoughts moved on to David and Aveena.

"Will you be moving on or staying another night Sir?" He hadn't noticed the receptionist approaching his table. She looked nice, in a red pencil skirt, a white blouse with a little gold badge saying 'Ms. Pat Goldsmith. Manager' She was about forty with a very slim figure, he suspected she only ate lettuce leaves and pasta.

"Probably." He paused for thought. "No, I will be staying another night."
"Thank you Sir." She replied as she scooped away his empty plate and moved the small dish of marmalade closer to him. Reg watched her walk away. Her black strappy high heels were just a quarter of an inch too high. She was a very dominant, confident lady, a manager.

The Culloden Tower was made of stone, quite high with a very tight spiral staircase. The views at the top were splendid, giving you an almost timeless vista of the small market town. Lunch was some sandwiches from a little cafe in the square. The museum was a homage to the TV program 'All creatures great and small' The James Herriot Vet program and lead mining. The TV program set instantly took him back to David and Aveena, - 'she wants a degree in Mammalogy, she wants to be a vet but money's an issue'. The Lead mining instantly took him to his cream and grey office. Lead thefts were almost a seasonal thing, usually just before Christmas there would be a spate of naked church roofs as the grey heavy gold got exchanged for notes at some dodgy scrapyard.

Time was creeping on. It was twenty five past four when he went into The Ship Inn. There were two people, Colin, who was busy wiping the shiny copper plated bar and David sitting in the corner by the window, the same as yesterday. David Smiled as Reg came in.

"Good afternoon Reg, let me get them in for you."
"Certainly not." Reg looked at David's glass, it was three quarters empty. "Do you have any mild on draught Landlord?"
"I've got something from the North Ridings Brewery but the name's a bit off putting."
"What is it?"
"Marshmallow Mild."
"See what you mean, I'll give it a go and a pint of shandy for young David over there please Colin." It was that strange, almost forced, friendliness that you were expected to adopt in a pub. He'd only known them both twenty four hours and already it was first name casualness as though they'd grown up together.

Reg waited at the bar whilst they were drawn. The lemonade came from an R. Whites bottle.

"There you go David." Reg put the two pint glasses down on the solid wood table top. It was impossible not to spill a little so two wet rings immediately formed around the base of the glasses, an unopened bag of cheese and onion crisps lay next to the ashtray.

"Had a good day? Issued twenty five tickets?" Reg jokingly asked.
"Well you see, therein lies the problem. I know most folk in the town so when they see me walking very slowly down a line of cars they very quickly move. Or, if they don't we have a little chat about the weather or their families, I point out the parking regulations and then they move."
"So how many tickets have you issued today?"

"Errr one. That was to a very rude young man who gave me a lot of verbals. If he'd just smiled and moved on I wouldn't have even clicked my biro."

"So it all depends on attitude and manners."

"Yes exactly." David took a large swig from the new pint.

"I have to get a new job Reg, I'm no good at this. The Inspector in the station is always calling me in and threatening me with the sack for lack of numbers. He thinks I'm lazy but I'm not."

"Well, it would be a great loss to this little town if you did. Just tell the inspector to go ahead, then tell the local press and you'll be surprised how many people would come out and support you. I've seen it happen before with a local village bobby down my way. They sent him to Hereford for three months 'refresher training' then gave him his job back. They had to, the public were in uproar."

"There are other factors Reg, I couldn't do that. Shall we open the crisps?"

"Are you sixty five then Reg? You don't look it."

"No, I'm sixty two, just had enough, stuck in an office with a computer. The highlight of my professional life was when the computer changed from muddy beige to functional black and the words changed from green to black and white. Had to get out, nothing mattered anymore, the world was in carnage, wars and killing going on everywhere and there I was writing a bulletin about lead being nicked off a church roof."

"Yeah but little things do matter Reg, if nobody cared about the lead the next thing to go would be the slates and then rape pillage and murder would be the norm. No, yours was a very important job."

"Maybe it's just me that wasn't important then."

"Does your wife love you?" The question David asked cut through all the flim-flam of social behaviour.

"Wow! What a question."

"I feel we are on a similar level Reg. You don't have to answer if I'm wrong."

Reg looked at David. 'Oh God! What had he done!' He thought.

"In answer to your question David, yes, I'm sure she does love me, but she doesn't respect me, thinks I'm off my trolley retiring early and doing what I'm doing. Hates my car, thinks it's vulgar, thinks I look stupid in my new clothes. But yes she loves me and I love her."

"You're a lucky man then Reg. What are you doing for food tonight?"

"No idea, haven't thought about it, probably walk about, see if there's a decent restaurant, failing that eat in the Hotel."

"Why don't you come home with me, eat at our place, Vanessa's cooking toad in the hole tonight and Aveena would love a new face to talk to, take her out of herself if you know what I mean."

Reg took a drink of the dark brown beer.

"Well thank you, that's very kind of you David. Are you sure?"

"Yes of course, there's always too much food, I usually end up eating it cold the next day."

"One for the road then?" Reg said.

"My shout." Said David.

"Not permitted. Sorry but you're providing the food, I'll provide the drink. Colin, have you got a half decent bottle of Merlot I can buy?"

Colin grunted from the small passageway that led back from the bar.

"No! I've got a very decent bottle of Merlot you can buy but it's expensive."

"How much?"

"A tenner."

That's OK, two more pints, a very decent bottle of Merlot and another bag of crisps please." Reg smiled at David. He wished he'd met him years ago.

The cold evening air felt refreshing as the beer softened their senses.

"Where's your car Reg?" David asked.

"At the hotel, I like to walk whenever I can, it helps me think and I need the exercise."

"Think about what?" David asked as they walked together.

"My shed."

"You think about your shed?"

Reg laughed.

"Of course, don't all men think about their sheds?"

"Do you think I should get a shed Reg?"

"Of course, you're not a complete man until you get a shed."

"Where's the Merlot from?" David asked.

"Chile."

"That's nice, I like red from Chile, it's not as bitter as the French stuff. Here we are, number sixteen." David opened the unlocked door of the front porch. It was small, only a couple of feet to the main front door which had a glazed half circle of leaded coloured glass panels in the style of a fan. He went to put his key in the lock but someone beat him to it. The door swung open and there she was.

Kathleen Thomas's face was indelibly etched into Reg's memory, white and terrified, flinching away as his bullet exploded the watermelon all over her, flinching the other way as the unseen meteoric bullet travelled past her head and into the wall. The enclosed violent noise, the smell, the smoke, his excitement, her fear. That moment.

Yet here she was, a beautiful flowering bud about to brighten every thing she touched, every place she went. Her skin was white and perfect, energy flowed from her body, her face, her eyes. Reg could see in an instant the happy face of Kathleen Thomas before he'd killed her.

"Reg, this is my daughter Aveena, she lights up my life and empties my wallet. Aveena this is Reg, a travelling poet I picked up in the pub."

Aveena was quicker than Reg in offering him her hand at the same time as casting scolding glances at her father. Reg automatically shook her gentle young hand, if he'd thought about it he couldn't have done it.

"Pleased to meet you Mr. ------------------?"
"Moorcroft, Reg Moorcroft."

The three of them entered the house. It was traditional, the stairs led off from the hallway, the lounge was the first room on the right, the dining room was the second door on the right and the kitchen was beyond at the end of the hall. All the woodwork was painted cream and the wallpaper was subtle roses. The pattern was a woman's choice. A woman popped her head out of the kitchen. She was tall and thin with dark hair just like David, but unlike David she didn't have a moustache.

She waved.

"Hi, I'm Vanessa, David's sister. Go into the dining room, food will only be ten minutes."

Reg walked towards her with the bottle of red.

"I grabbed this from the pub, no idea if it's good or not,"

Vanessa looked at him then at the bottle.

"Looks OK, are you really a travelling poet?"
"No, I'm a retired Crime Analyst from Hereford Police Station just travelling around to places I've never been to before, taking a few photos and writing a few lines as the fancy takes me."
"Oh, that sounds very romantic, are you travelling in a Gypsy Caravan pulled by a gentle but strong horse that you talk to?"
"No, a Vauxhall." They both laughed as she struggled with the bottle opener.
"Here, you can do this, it's a man's job."

"Not sure if I'm a man, I'll have to check." They both laughed again.
"Go through, it'll be about five minutes."
"OK."

Reg walked through into the small but homely dining room. There was an oval oak gateleg table and four matching straight back chairs with tapestry upholstery. An old fashioned fireplace with a large framed picture of Kathleen Thomas on the wall above it. He was to spend the next few hours eating with her family whilst she looked on from above the mantelpiece. Reg decided that you couldn't possibly make up such a bizarre situation. Maybe the wine would calm him.

It was the way she moved that captivated him. He'd forgotten how young people could move so fast, so effortlessly. The gift of years was a trade off for unnoticeable slow decline. She wasn't overtly pretty but her youth unavoidably showered everything in joyful light.

"Where do you live Mr. Moorcroft?" Her girl's voice, so easy on the ear.
"Please call me Reg. In the countryside in Herefordshire, just in England, I shop in Wales."
"What shop?" Reg looked at her. Her dark matter of fact hair only served to make her skin look whiter, her dark framed glasses only served to make her hazel eyes look bigger.
"Waitrose or Marks and Spencers."
"Not Tescos or the Coop?"
"Never." She was measuring him, deciding if he was for real.

The food came and Vanessa sat down with them. David poured the wine, Aveena didn't want any. It was very obvious that David, Vanessa and Aveena were related. The food, especially the sausages, was delicious. The wine mellowed the three adults.

"So Aveena, what's your plan?"
"Become a mammalogist, and study Gobi Bears and Snow leopards in the Gobi desert. If I could also find a few dinosaur eggs it would be a bonus."
"Didn't know there was a Gobi bear." Reg said after another sip of wine.
"There's only about thirty to forty left in the wild, they're smaller than Panda's."
"It's in her dreams Reg, she knows the financial situation." David put his napkin down on his empty plate.
"We all need dreams David. Reg half sang the words:-

'You've got to have a dream,

If you don't have a dream,
How you gonna have a dream come true! Bom! Bom!

"Where's that from uncle Reg?" Her use of the word surprised and pleased him. He noticed that Vanessa and David also noticed.

"It's from a song called 'Happy Talk' which is from the musical 'South Pacific', a Rodgers and Hammerstein musical, before your time Aveena."
"I'm going to find it on a cassette."
"If you can find that Aveena, I'll pay for it." Laughed David.
"Yes and I'll listen to it." Added Vanessa.
"More wine Reg?" Vanessa asked.
"Yes please."
"Which is the best university to study Mammalogy Aveena?" Reg asked.
"Bristol, don't know if you watch animal documentaries but most of them, including the David Attenborough ones are made by BBC West which is Bristol. It seems to be the UK centre for anything nature, animals or wildlife so the uni there seems to be the training ground for that type of person."
"That's only an hour away from where I live. I live in the Wye Valley, it's rather beautiful." The wine was making him mellow, he wanted to offer there and then to fund her through uni but stopped short. It was far too early.
"That was a magnificent meal Vanessa. If I wasn't married I'd marry you tomorrow just for your cooking."
"Just for my cooking?" She laughed.
"Have you got any money?"
"A little bit."
"Well your money as well then." She wrapped his knuckles with a large serving spoon. Everyone laughed.
"She's loaded." David said. Took her husband to the cleaners when they got divorced. You be very careful Reg, she's a very dangerous woman."
"All women are dangerous, aren't they Aveena?" Reg pointed the question. Aveena blushed and coiled back.
"I'm not, I just prefer little mammals to boys."
"Sensible, very sensible." Reg said and everyone laughed again.

Vanessa got up and collected up the plates, after about five minutes she came back with a large apple crumble.

"Custard or cream Reg?" Vanessa asked, serving to everyone.

"Has to be custard, everytime!"

"I bet you like cold custard out of the fridge?" Vanessa smiled.

"Are you always so perceptive about men?"

"Always!"

It was gone ten when Reg said his goodbyes.

"Where are your travels taking you next week?" Vanessa asked as he reached for his leather jacket.

"Holmfirth, going to do the 'Last of the Summer Wine' tour."

"That's not that far away from here, why don't you pop by for another meal, we all love to hear your 'Police' stories and I'm doing a Lancashire Hotpot."

Reg checked in with David.

"Yes please do." David said. "It's been a great evening, really brightened up our dull lives. Please come."

"But here is Yorkshire." Reg replied.

"That's OK, just don't tell anyone." Vanessa giggled.

Aveena tugged his arm.

"See you next Wednesday then uncle Reg." She was so young, so vibrant, why stand still when you can bounce.

"What wine goes with Lancashire Hotpot?" Reg asked as he moved from the porch onto the short front drive.

"A nice red Bordeaux or Cabernet Sauvignon would be nice." Vanessa chirped in.

Reg looked at her in the borrowed light of the hall.

"Bit sophisticated your sister David."

"Yes, she's been around a bit." Vanessa kicked out at him.

The walk back to the hotel was a jumble of thoughts and sensations. It was almost grotesque his intentional targeting of her family. Trying to right a wrong, trying to pour thick oil over the troubled waters of the past. They were lovely, friendly, welcoming people, she must have been the same. David was so lucky to have a daughter like Aveena. He hadn't been aware of how big the hole in their lives was until now, it was huge, a daughter like Aveena would have filled it with light, movement and fun. How could he explain that to Rosamund?

It was just before eleven when he got back to the hotel. Everything was just about to shut. He didn't normally drink but tonight was different, the wine had eased his normal caution. He ordered a double whisky with just a tiny shot of water from the closing bar and sat in one of the comfortable armchairs sipping and swilling it around the chunky heavy square glass. The thin male night receptionist came over.

"Will you be wanting to stay another night, Sir?"

"No, leaving in the morning after I've had one of your excellent breakfasts."

The thin young man smiled.

"OK. I'll have your bill made up, it will be waiting in reception tomorrow morning. Will you be wanting anything else from the bar?"

"No thanks, I'm off to bed in a moment"

He'd bring some money with him next week. He'd no idea how much was left. In fact he'd no idea how much there'd been in the first place, he'd never counted it. The money was stashed at the bottom of an old Duckhams five gallon oil drum in the corner of the shed with a pile of rags on top. Last week he'd left the door open in the sunshine and later, when he went back in, he found one of Doug's bloody hens sitting on the pile of rags. She got quite ratty when he shoo'd her out. She was beautiful mind, all subtle reds, browns and gold. She looked at him as hens do, cocking her head to one side and giving him the evil glare.

The road back south was just a road, background music to his thoughts.

Rosamunds blue Beetle was at the top of the drive, he didn't want to block her in as sometimes she wanted to go shopping late in the afternoon.

"I'm back." He shouted up the stairs.

"Well that's a relief, put the kettle on love, I'll be down in a minute, just tidying the airing cupboard."

Sophia the cat immediately fussed around his legs, rubbing up against his jeans and purring for food.

"Did you write your poem?" She asked as she came down.

"Yes."

"Can I see it?"

"No! It's rubbish, poems only mean things to the writer, other people just don't get it."

She took his bag from his hand.

"Where's your lunchbox?"

"In the bag. Any post?"

"Only the usual stuff, bank and bills. Sit down, I'll make the tea, are you hungry? What do you fancy?"

"Fish fingers mash and peas."

"You're easy to please Reg Moorcroft, is there a hidden side to you?"

"Oh yes, my hidden side would have demanded a Lancashire hotpot."

"Glad he's hidden then." she pecked him on the cheek. "The grass needs cutting."

"Rosamund, stop beating around the bush, just come out with it, say what you mean, the grass needs cutting. I get it!" It was the sort of humour that only came with marriage. "Tomorrow if it's not raining." He settled into the corner of the sofa, she brought his tea in then left for the kitchen. Sophia still fussed around his legs.

Rosamund always spent Saturday mornings in town. Savoury ducks and pork pie from Hancocks, cherry tomatoes, bag of watercress and custard pies from Marks and Spencers sometimes a lemon meringue, then shopping from Waitrose.

He'd christened the golden speckled hen 'Molly' he had no idea why, but Molly was always trying to get into his shed. He didn't really mind, she was very cute but she did tend to shit everywhere then eye you up as much as to say 'What?' Reg lifted the rags from the top of the oil drum. He'd bought the drum years ago when he had a Mini Metro and used to do his own oil changes but changing the oil filter was fiddly and messy so after all the oil was used up he cut the top off the drum and carefully hammered the sharp edges down. He'd found it quite satisfying. Now the drum was an integral part of his shed. Reg counted out twenty thousand pounds and put the rags back. There was still a lot left in the drum. He put the cash into a stout dark green Marks and Spencers bag that had come full of grey socks, took it around the house and put it into the glove box of the Carlton. It was full of tape cassettes. He looked at the top one. David Bowie, Hunky Dory. He'd play that on the way up North on Monday. He had no excuse, he'd put it off for two days, blaming the weather. Reg got the mower out of the garage.

Roast lamb with new potatoes and mint sauce. They sat and ate the delicious meal almost in silence. If they'd had a daughter like Aveena there would have been noise, comments, conversation, laughter, young energy that would have bounced between them. Reg thought it but said nothing. Rosamund picked up on his quietness.

"Penny for them?"
Reg smiled.
"Thinking about 'Last of the Summer Wine.' I'm going to head for Holmfirth on Monday, see what sort of rubbish I can write when I'm actually in the same location as my hero."
"Who's your hero?"
"Clegg."
"I'd have thought it would have been 'Compo' knowing the deep affection you have for your 'wellies'."
"See, you don't know everything about me. I'm a mystery man."
Rosamund looked at him.
"You certainly are Reg Morrcroft. You certainly are. Lamb OK?"
"Delicious. I'm thinking of changing my car again."

Rosamund was taken back.

"Why, I thought you liked the green monster."

"I do but the clutch is just too heavy for everyday use, thinking of getting one of those new Honda Jazz."

"You never cease to amaze me. Can't say I'm sad, never did like that car, too big and ugly."

"What's for pudding?"

"Just a yogurt."

"Is it Greek style?"

"Yes, vanilla, full fat."

"I take it back, you do know everything about me."

Reg wondered what would be in his sandwiches as cold lamb didn't really work. He was excited by the thought of Holmfirth but more excited by the thought of spending an evening with Aveena and her family. Just to watch her was a joy. It was the power of her youth, so clean and unblemished by sordid, squalid, nasty life. The lotus Carlton seemed eager to climb the motorways North, as though Reg had to constantly rein it in. God he'd miss this car but it was the only way he could explain to Rosamund how he'd managed to fund Aveena's University degree. When the time came, that is.

For the second time David Bowie sang about 'Changes'.

Still don't know what I was looking for
And my time was running wild
A million dead-end streets
Every time I thought I'd got it made
It seemed the taste was not so sweet
So I turned myself to face me
But I've never caught a glimpse
Of how the others must see the faker
I'm much too fast to take that test

It seemed to fit his situation exactly. He wouldn't be quite so fast in a 'Jazz' though and he wasn't so sure about Leo Thrust. He'd never be seen dead in a 'Jazz'. No Leo would have to die.

He stopped at some awful bleak tatty services to use the toilet. He couldn't resist a peep. Pork pie, tomatoes, a little bit of mustard in some cling film, an apple and a yogurt. He'd eat it when he got to the 'Holmfirth' road sign.

It was raining, it always was on Monday mornings especially as you headed North. The plan was skirt around the eastern side of Mamchester and then a right onto the A635 and the galloping open spaces of the moors. He thought of Allan Mayor now, a permanent fixture in his office. Bright, sharp, more bulletins coming out than coffees going in. 'Do you remember Reg Moorcroft?" People would say. ' and his silly Monday morning tales, they were funny, Allan's so serious about everything. Even his updates on the baby are serious.' They'd say. Reg consciously throttled back as the lotus had quietly crept up to eighty five.

The sign was a traditional black and white rectangle with two thirds of a circle on the top. It was a bit like a black and white etching, the square church tower and it's surrounding buildings sitting on top of 'Welcome to' then Holmfirth running the length of the sign. It was raining quite heavily now so Reg dropped the passenger's window and snapped from the car. There was no indication of it's real claim to fame as being the backdrop to a ridiculous television programme about three old men, released from their life obligations slowly but irretrievably sliding backwards to their childhood. Their boyhood.

Was that what he was doing? Being a boy, roaming about, discovering fascinating things like how many times do you have to hit a snail with a stone before it's shell breaks or how far will a worm stretch before it breaks into two worms. Or perhaps it was enough just to not have to be competitive. The pork pie was delicious, they always were, he especially loved the clear jelly stuff. He started to think about a poem as he stared at the first wet bleak stone buildings through the rivulets that ran down the screen. Then he thought about David, Vanessa and Aveena. It was a bit 'crass' just to hand over a bag with twenty thousand pounds. Perhaps he'd broach the subject, see how it went down and if it was good, go to the Uni and offer to pay all the fees up front. Yes, that was much more sensible.

You couldn't really miss Syd's Cafe or the famous steps Nora Batty defended so gallantly against the scruffy little man in wellies. Of course Clegg was the voice of reason sandwiched between the two extremes of an incompetent Sargeant Major and a street urchin. It was a bit like his old job really, the smart cleanliness of the Police Service and the dirt of low level life. The roads were black and wet, the stone of the buildings were black on the top fading to sand colour at the bottom. He'd write it in Syd's cafe.

"Tea and a Lardy cake please."
"That'll do your figure no good at all." The forty something waitress with no waist but a lovely smile said.
"Do you think I need to worry about my figure at my age?"
"Of course." Her smile broadened, Reg smiled back.

"I suppose you're waiting for three of your mates to come along?"
"Of course!." He said, they both chuckled.
"Which is 'THE' table?" Reg asked.
"That one there but as you can see it's occupied."
"In that case I'll sit by the window and watch the weather."
"Sit down, I'll bring it over."

It was just like the TV show only there were no 'Lights, Camera, Action, or super cool young people fussing about. In fact it was quite peaceful with only five people in the cafe.

"Next week it all starts again. Madness if you ask me? How can three childish old men be so interesting? They do nothing." She put his tea and cake down then left before he could say anything.

It reminded Reg of the words

Busy doing nothing,
Working the whole day through,
Trying to find
Lot's of things not to do!

He wasn't sure which song they were from. The Lardy cake was delicious.

And so it seems the rain never stops,
If you wait for the dry to smile
The sun to warm your style
Then you'll wait for a while.

So grin and bear it,
Put on a mac
Put up your brolly
And go to the shop
Cause the rain will never stop.

I'm in a town where the men are called peter,
Cause their lives have all gone down the pan
Chasing that naughty tinkerbell
Trying to be strong like a man.

Captain Hook is the tallyman
He counts you in and out
A house, a car, a wife some kids
Sometimes a man has to shout.

Take away the accounts,
Give me a comic
I don't want twin carbs
I want a bike
Marbles on the pavement
And marvellous cards
I can look at for hours
And never get bored.
Somehow the rain was just showers.

Reg chuckled at his attempt, ripped off the notelet and put it into his hat.

"Do you know anywhere decent I can stay the night?" Reg called to the passing waitress.
"Do you want decent, cheap or decent expensive?"
She had blondish light brown hair that didn't quite manage to reach her shoulders and didn't quite manage to be curly. Bit of a mess really, but somehow it went with her and the place.
"Well I like a bit of comfort."
"The Huntsman Inn."
"I think I passed that on the way in."
"Did you come in from Manchester?"
"Yes."
"Then you would have. My sister works there, it's as good as you get round here, that'll be one pound seventy please."
Reg shoved his hand into the jeans pocket. That was the only snag with his new jeans, they were a tight fit so it was difficult to put your hand in the pocket. He stood up to make it easier.
"Nice Jacket." The woman said.
"It's a Belstaff."
"Looks like a motorbike jacket."
Reg gave her the money.

There was nothing else to see in Holmfirth, everything was tainted with the show, the steep stone walls of the river bank looked exactly like they did on the TV. The sloping steep narrow lanes lined with old cold blackened stone led to Syd's cafe. He half expected an old zinc bath on four pram wheels to come hurtling down. But it didn't. It was just a diversion anyway. His thoughts were in Richmond.

The Huntsman Inn was made of stone. The restaurant was nice with a timbered roof filled in with plain white board. Somehow nothing mattered, he drank half a bottle of a nice nameless white wine with his fish then went to a comfortable bed.

How would he handle tomorrow? How would it go, if it went well, what about Rosamund? When should he talk about Aveena? Should he ever talk about her? Should he turn around tomorrow, go back home, sell the car and dig out his old car coat? Nobody knew anything about anything, for Gods sake stop before it was too late. Let the cat out of the bag, the genie out of the bottle, open the flood gates. He stared out of the window, there was a large sodium light somewhere on the wall that made the falling rain look like rivulets of gold. He wished he could talk to his mother, she'd died early, only sixty four. He could remember that day vividly, a phone call at four in the morning, his dad choking back the tears 'I'd fallen asleep in the chair, when I woke up, she'd gone.' As though he'd failed her at the very moment she needed him most. He'd just got in the car and driven the two and half hours to the little street house. Rosamund had wanted to come with him but it would have taken too long by the time she'd washed, dressed and done her hair, 'made herself decent' she would have called it but it would have taken an hour and he wanted to be with dad as soon as he could. It nearly caused an argument.

Reg knew what his mother would say anyway - 'let sleeping dogs lie', but he couldn't, he had to do his best.

Bleak was the most appropriate word for the Yorkshire Moors, The car took him eastward very quickly, it wasn't far to Richmond. He'd kick around to four-ish and meet up with David in the pub.

"You made it then?" David smiled as Reg walked into the Ship Inn. Colin nodded towards the Newcastle Brown pump.
"No, I'll have a Guinness for a change." Reg said. "Yes I made it David, can't stay away from the place."
"Where've you been this week?"
"Holmfirth."
"Not much to see there is there?"

"No."

"Did you write a poem?"

"Yes." Colin's ears pricked up at the comment as he reassessed his colourfully dressed customer.

"Yes, that fits, one pound twenty five please."

Reg paid him.

"Any wine tonight?"

"Wait." Reg commanded. "What are we eating tonight David?"

David put his shandy down.

"Plaice and parsley sauce I think."

"Do you have a decent Chardonnay Bartender?"

"I do."

"Then I'll take it, yes I know it's expensive." Reg preempted the coming remark.

"So how many tickets have you issued so far this week?" Reg asked, putting the dark Irish Stout down on the table.

"Three, it could have been four but it was a really old bloke who didn't know how to put money in the meter. You just can't be that nasty can you?"

"No you can't. Another Shandy?"

"Yes OK."

"Crisps."

"Yes OK." Reg noticed that David was sitting uncomfortably, as though one side of his body was rigid.

"Ms. Vanessa, what a pleasure to meet you again." Reg took her hand, bowed slightly, raised her hand and kissed it.

"You Southern men are so full of twaddle; but I love it. Very nice to see you again Mr. Moorcroft." Everybody laughed.

"No Aveena?" Reg asked.

"She'll be back in about half an hour, she's gone to the library."

"Supper smells good."

"Fresh fillet of plaice this morning from Grimsby docks."

"And?" Reg inquired.

"Peas, asparagus, button mushrooms done in a sauce and Guernesey new potatoes."

"And a bottle of Colin's best Chardonnay to complement your exquisite meal."

"Who's Colin?" Vanessa asked.

"The Barman at the Ship."

"Oh!"

It was twenty minutes before Aveena let herself in the front door. It was the speed and ease of her every movement that captivated Reg. 'Youth is wasted on the young' was so true' he thought as she slid effortlessly onto the chair by the table.

"So! What have you got?" It seemed so easy to talk to her, she made the past almost irrelevant.
"A Field Guide to the Mammals of Mongolia and The King of the Gobi - The story of the Wild Bactrian Camel". She beamed at him across the table. "Can't wait! What's for tea Aunt Ness?"

Vanessa shouted through from the kitchen "Fish but mushroom soup first.".

"Best china soup bowls, blimey we must be expecting an important visitor, any idea who it is Uncle Reg?" Aveena giggled.
"No idea, but this soup is delicious." Reg poured the wine.

There was no mistaking it. Everytime David moved the spoon to within an inch or two of his lips the tremor set in. The napkin was a necessity. Reg noticed it, Vanessa and Aveena noticed that he'd noticed.

"Oh for goodness sake. Dad's got early onset Parkinsons, he's in denial but everybody knows."

David slammed down his napkin.

"Aveena!" He almost shouted then instantly lowered his voice. "Reg is a guest, he doesn't want to know our problems. Now let's enjoy our meal." There was an awkward silence.
"You've worked with the Police Uncle Reg. tell him he should take a medical retirement before he has an accident." There was another pause.
"She's right David, you should retire."
"And do what? Wait to die, I've looked into it Reg, the pension would only be about two thirds of my salary. We can't live on that."
"David, I'm going to be blunt here, issuing three tickets a week, they're going to sack you before long. Take the medical and retire quickly."
"I'll get a job at Marks and Sparks Dad, we'll be OK." Aveena chipped in.
"No you won't Aveena." Everyone turned and looked at Reg.
"I'm or rather my wife and I are going to fund your degree at Bristol Uni. We've discussed it." He lied. We're comfortably off with no kids and I'm damned if I'm going to

leave what we've got to the tax man or some charity with an overpaid C.E.O. "I've researched the course and the first year has been paid for." He lied again.

There was stunned silence.

"Now I'm going to be blunt." David said. "Reg, we hardly know you and you hardly know us. We're two blokes who met in a pub. You just don't do things like this. It doesn't happen in real life. Please just forget you ever said that. After this meal we'll probably never see you again and that won't matter cause you're not part of our world. Now let's just eat up and enjoy."

Vanessa jumped to her feet.

"David Thomas ,unless you accept this kind man's wonderful offer to give your daughter the chance of her lifetime I will never ever cook or care for you again." She sat down panting and breathless. He knew she meant it.

Aveena looked at her father.

"Please Dad, it's what I really want."

David Thomas picked up his thrown down napkin and wiped his chin.

"Looks as though I'm out voted Reg. I don't know what to say."
"Don't say anything David, ring in sick tomorrow morning then get yourself to the doctors, a few months on the sick and they'll be more than happy to give you a medical retirement. I know, I've seen it many times from officers with bad backs. What's for pudding Vanessa?"
"Lemon Meringue."
"Did you make it?"
"No, Marks and Spencers but I put it in the oven, does that count?"
"Most definitely, that's the most crucial part." Everybody laughed.

Reg pointed the car south towards the M1. He disliked going the same way as coming so it was circular hoop, Leeds. Sheffield, Nottingham, Birmingham then crosscountry to the Marches. It was effortless in the big powerful car except in a jam or a queue when the effort of pressing the clutch made his left leg ache. He'd go and exchange it next week for a Jazz, Rosamund would like that, he'd take her with him to choose the colour. The released cash would be handy to legitimately pay for Aveena's course. That is after he'd told Rosamund about his plans. That could be tricky. Reg rummaged in the cassette pile, 'The Police' 'Walking on the Moon' that would do for a while. He'd turn off at the next services, have a cup of tea, maybe a cake, no, a pasty or pie and have a rummage through the drum of cheap cassettes, there always was one, sometimes you could find something good.

Chapter 11.

Reg and Rosamund sat on their usual ends of the big blue sofa with Sophia between them. The nine o'clock news was about to start.

"Have you got a girlfriend or another woman?" Rosamund calmly asked without taking her gaze from the TV. "Your little trips are getting longer and longer."

Reg put his cup down on the carpet, picked up the remote, clicked off the TV and turned to face her. Rosamund stayed staring at the black screen fearful that what was coming would wreck her life.

"I met a bloke called David in a pub in a place called Richmond in North Yorkshire. He's a Traffic Warden. We had a few pints together then he invited me to his home, just a normal three bedroomed semi, for a meal. It's quite a sad story, his wife died a while back, heart attack then slipped into a coma from which she never recovered. Anyway it turns out that David has early onset Parkinsons, he's only thirty nine. They have a daughter, she's seventeen, called Aveena. She's mad about animals, wants to be a vet. She's bright as a button, straight A's at school. She desperately wants to go to Uni for a degree in mammalogy but her dad spent all the family savings on his wife's funeral so Aveena's resigned herself to her dad taking a medical retirement and her working in Marks and Spencers to help with the bills. Anyway I said I'd pay for her to do a degree at Bristol Uni, apparently it's the best place for animal stuff. Aveena wants to go to the Gobi Desert in Mongolia to study bears."

There was an awful silence. Reg had no idea what to expect.

Rosamund took a deep breath in.

"Well I'll give you this Reg Moorcroft, you couldn't make that one up. You met a bloke in a pub, miles from home, and you've decided to give all our money to his daughter so that she can go to Mongolia to look at bears. I suppose you're aware that Paddington made it all the way from Peru without a penny of our money."

"I'm going to get rid of the Vauxhall next week, I know you hate it, I'm going to buy a new Honda Jazz, come with me to look at it, you can choose the colour then with the cash I get back from the deal I'm going to fund Aveena."

"Don't you think we should have talked all this through Reg before you committed anything."

"No, you'd have talked me out of it, and I'm glad I did it. Let's face it Rosamund we're comfortably off and we're not getting any younger. I'm certainly not leaving my money to any of my family and you haven't got any family. I want to invite her down to meet you. How would you feel about that?"

"Well I suppose it's one step removed from 'another woman, a mistress'. Do you want another cup of tea?"
"OK, shall I feed the cat? Reg asked.
"No, I need to think."

Rosamund was a good ten minutes tidying up the kitchen, emptying the tumble dryer and feeding Sophia. She came back into the lounge, went over to him and kissed his bald head.

"What was that for?"
"Sorry." She said quietly.
"Sorry what for?"
"Sorry for not giving you the daughter you would have loved and spoiled rotten."
Rosamund sat on her end of the sofa and put out her hand for him to hold.
"Put the TV back on Reg, we'll watch the ten'o o'clock news and weather then go to bed."
"Yes OK."
"I'd like a nice red one."
"Red what"
"A red Honda Jazz."
"Red's a terrible colour, in the sun it just fades."
"I don't care."
"Red it is then." He looked at his wife of twenty three years and decided he loved her very much.

"Where are we going?" Rosamund asked as she reluctantly got into the large brutal Vauxhall.

"Shirley Road Solihull, Listers Garage."

"What's that beeping?"

"You need to put your seatbelt on."

"Is it all arranged?"

"All arranged." Reg replied, reaching out and squeezing her hand. "Pick a cassette from the glove box, it'll calm you down and make the journey go quicker."

"How do you know I need to calm down?"

Reg looked across at her, they both smiled. She chose 'The Best of Matt Monro'.

At sixty eight miles per hour the Lotus was almost silent. There was the usual build up of traffic from the M5 along the Quinton Expressway and towards the ring road. Reg had to admit to himself the little Jazz with it's featherweight clutch would be a much easier car in town. A bit buzzy on the motorway though.

The young boy salesman, actually he was probably early twenties but Reg perceived him as a boy. Couldn't wait to get behind the wheel of the Lotus and drive it out of Reg's life behind a big grey shed. In the showroom an older lizard handed him two sets of keys, all the paperwork, a cheque for twenty three thousand pounds and a 'Listers of Solihull' tax disc holder.

"It's waiting for you outside Sir, full of petrol and ready to go. Thank you very much for your custom and remember we're always here to help."

Rosamund and Reg walked outside into the grey Birmingham late morning. Reg was carrying a plastic bag full of his cassettes and bit's and bobs. The bright red Jazz was sitting on it's own at the end of the lot.

"How much was it Reg? It looks very nice, very modern."

"Twelve thousand pounds." He could hear Rosamunds brain whirring.

"So your little year of enjoyment has cost us ten thousand pounds."

Reg shrugged his shoulders.

"You're a long time dead Rosamund." Reg pressed the key fob and the little car chirped into life. They both got in. This time Rosamund was a lot closer to him. It smelt like all modern new cars. Plastic and more plastic. The clutch almost gave up with just the weight of his loake shoe. Reg took off his cap as it just didn't feel right in the car. His leather jacket now just got in the way of everything. Leo Thrust was dead.

"Do you want to stop somewhere for lunch?" Reg asked.

"No, let's just go home Reg." She could sense her husband's disappointment at having, driving, being seen in, such an eminently practical sensible vehicle. He was cream and grey again.

The road north was now laborious. Everything worked fine, it was really good on petrol, but somehow the cassette player just wasn't made for David Bowie or Otis Redding. Radio two worked fine and when he bored of 'PAP' music there was always the thinking man's entertainment - Radio 4. Still the thought of the journey back with Aveena sitting beside him cheered him up.

David was off sick. He'd visibly deteriorated since his last visit three weeks ago. Vanessa had moved in as his carer, drawing a small secret salary from Reg.

Reg parked on the front drive and knocked the little brass knocker. It had been recently polished with brasso the white powder residue clung to the dark blue paint. Vanessa answered the door.

"Hello handsome stranger, please come in."

"Well that's a first."

"What?"

"Being called handsome, lots of folk have said I'm strange though." They both laughed as he entered the little comfortable semi.

"Is my passenger ready to go?"

"She's been ready for the last week. Come in Reg, I've cooked a meal, you must rest and eat before you leave."

"What have you cooked?"

"Liver and onions, mashed spuds, carrots and cabbage."

"Will you marry me Vanessa?"

"Of course, I thought you'd never ask." She grabbed his coat as he took it off then grabbed his arm leading him through to the dining room. David came out of the living room to greet him. His walking was now more of a shuffle.

"I can't believe you've come to steal my beautiful daughter Reg Moorcroft, that's the last time that I'll talk to a strange man in a pub."

Reg turned to Vanessa.

"See, I told you I get called strange - a lot." David held out his shaking hand, Reg took it and steadied it. Reg could hear Aveena bouncing down the stairs.

"Just tell me again, when are you bringing her back?"

"Not sure, probably Tuesday or Wednesday, the plan is a 'get to know you' weekend with Rosamund , then I'll take her down to Bristol for an interview at the Uni. On the other hand it could be in ten years time, when she's about to get married 'cause I'm not paying for her Uni and her wedding."

"Are you sure about that, Uncle Reg?" Aveena chipped in.

"No."

"No wine Reg?" Vanessa commented as she brought the food through.

"No, wouldn't look good would it? 'Sixty two year old retired crime analyst with very little hair arrested for drunken driving whilst kidnapping a seventeen year old girl from Richmond.'

You can just imagine it! When questioned by Police Moorcroft said, "I'm just taking her to school in Bristol! That smells delicious Vanessa."

Her tears were a mixture of excitement and sorrow as she hugged and kissed her father goodbye. David Thomas was also in tears. He'd lost his wife, he'd never work again and now his wonderful daughter was leaving. Reg knew what he was feeling.

"It's only for a few days David, I'll bring her back safely."

"I know, I know, but if it all goes well, what then? One day she'll leave and not come back."

"Daughters never leave their Dad's David. You should know that." Reg squoze David's shoulder.

In the hall was her bag, it was a small blue backpack with zips everywhere. Reg picked it up, there wasn't much in it.

Then she was beside him. The little car nimbly threaded it's way out of the town and towards the motorway.

"Put some music on if you want." Reg said.

"What have you got?"

"All sorts,have a look in the glove box."

Aveena sorted through the tapes.

"It's all a bit old uncle Reg."

"I'm old, what do you expect?"

"Cliff Richard, how about that?" She asked.

"I'm OK with it, more Rosamunds taste than mine, she went to see him at the local church, not singing of course, well he did sing but just hymns. Apparently he's very religious. Not married - never married." Reg added.

They both sang along when it came on.

"Travellin light, travellin light,
No comb and no toothbrush,
I got nothing to hide. I'm carryin only
A pocketful of dreams,
A heart full of love,
And they weigh nothin at allllllllll."

Reg and Aveena burst out laughing.

"I can see why you want to be a vet." Reg said.
"What do you mean?"
"Well I don't think you should consider a singing career."

Aveena hit his arm and turned the volume up as Cliff launched into 'Miss You Nights'.
She wound back the chair, put her feet up on the dash and thought about her Mom and
Dad. Reg didn't mind at all. David was so lucky having a daughter.

"I'm a bit scared about meeting your wife." She said quietly as they took a slip road to
join the M5.
"Well don't be, Rosamund's a wonderful person and to be honest she's just as nervous
about meeting you. As you know we've never had a family so being around children,
especially teenage children is a bit daunting for her."
"Can we stop for a break uncle Reg, there's some services coming up."
"Yes OK." Reg welcomed the suggestion, the little engine was busy buzzing away
working hard to keep up with the flow of traffic which was moving between seventy five
to eighty miles per hour. If it had been the Carlton he wouldn't have noticed any noise.

It was four in the afternoon when Reg turned the little red car into his drive. Rosamunds
blue beetle was at the top of the drive. Reg got stiffly out after the long journey perched
on the small driver's seat. Aveena got out slowly, nervously but effortlessly. Rosamund
was waiting at the front door, smiling.

"Hello you two. Hello Aveena." Rosamund said as she gave her a little polite hug. "Come on in." Aveena was nervous, Reg could see her looking around trying to take everything in.

"How was your journey in Reg's new car?"

"It was fine, Mr. Moorcroft is a very good driver and the new car is very nice."

"Call him Reg, everybody else does. Now come on upstairs, I'll show you your room." Aveena followed Rosamund upstairs.

"Actually I've been calling him 'Uncle Reg', is that OK, I know he's not my uncle but he's being very kind to me and my family so 'Uncle Reg' seems to fit."

"How about 'Aunty Rosamund'?"

Aveena and Rosamund looked at each other.

"That seems to fit too." Rosamund squoze Aveena's hand, she couldn't remember the last time there'd been a teenage girl in the house.

"That's a lovely blouse, where did you get it?"

"Tammy Girl', my aunt Vanessa brought it for my birthday. Dad paid for it of course but aunt Vanessa came with me to choose and buy it. Dad's unwell, do you know?"

"Yes Reg told me, sounds as though your family is going through a tough time."

"It's not easy. Aunt Vanessa's divorced so she's moved in and is looking after dad, he's had to give up work of course, not that he liked the job, he's far too nice and easy going. Uncle Reg said he would have been sacked anyway for not issuing enough tickets."

"And you?"

"All set for a job in M&S till uncle Reg came into our lives. I still can't believe it. It feels like a dream and I'm going to wake up soon in a greenish overall sitting behind a beeping till saying 'have a nice day' to smelly dirty fat men with snot dripping out of their nose on a cold day."

Rosamund and Aveena burst into laughter. Rosamund had put a small display of spring flowers in her room.

"Oh it's lovely and just look at the view."

"It's only our neglected back garden with Reg's shed, a field and Doug's wandering chickens next door."

"I've got a factory in front of my window."

"How about tomorrow we have a girls shopping afternoon in Cheltenham?"

Aveena hesitated.

"I haven't actually got a lot of money with me."

"Don't be silly, you can pretend to be my daughter and I can spoil you. Never had the chance before."

Aveena started to bounce.

"I've never been to Cheltenham, is it nice?"

"Shopping heaven. Come on better go down stairs and make him a cup of tea. Just egg and beans on toast for tea is that OK?"

"My favourite."

Rosamund and Aveena skipped down the stairs almost at the same speed.

Reg was sitting on his end of the sofa with Sophia sitting on his lap padding, purring and pulling at his jumper. He was watching the news whilst automatically stroking her. They came into the lounge almost together like two excited school girls.

"So what are you two up to?" Reg asked.

"Can't say it's a 'girl thing'." Rosamund admonished him for asking.

"That usually means it's going to cost me money."

"Of course but you do get egg and beans on toast and a cup of tea."

"Oh! That's OK then." It was as though a warm spring breeze scented with delicate flowers had whooshed into the house and filled every space. Rosamund and Aveena just wouldn't shut up.

"Never been in one of these new Beetles before, they're so cool." Avena said as she slipped onto the front passenger seat."

"Yes I like it, Reg doesn't, he says the front dash is ridiculously large, just so they could get the old Beetle shape. He's right of course but I don't care."

Rosamund and Aveena drove off in comfortable silence leaving Reg to mow the back lawn.

"Any children?" Aveena asked as they approached a bit of a queue before a traffic island. Rosamund looked at her as the car inched along.

"None of our own, my sisters got some but no, it just never happened for Reg and I. We both would have liked a daughter but there you go, that's life." There was a lot of sadness in Rosamunds voice and a hint of a moist tear. "Oh bother I forgot to tell him."

"Forgot what."

"Molly, one of Doug's chickens has got into his shed again, she shits everywhere, it drives him mad, it's his fault, he forgets to shut the door properly. We'll try Hobbs first."

"What for?"

"Some nice things for you. I've got loads of clothes, hardly ever wear half of them, never had the chance to buy things for a daughter so humour me."

They both giggled as the slip road for Cheltenham approached.

Aveena was a wonderful girl. Rosamund loved just looking at her as she slipped in and out of changing cubicles, some with a door, some with a curtain, all with a mirror. It was her shape, it was only there if you were seventeen, her bottom created a gap around her waist. A blouse or skinny jumper could dive into and still leave space to spare before her upper body became a perfect triangle.

"Shall we have a coffee and bun in Selfridges?" Rosamund suggested. By now both Rosamund and Aveena were cluttered with thick almost cardboard carrier bags with names all over them.
"Ooh, yes please." Rosamund was beginning to flag but Aveena had the energy of youth. She had to be careful with cakes and the like as they seemed to immediately attach themselves to her waistline. Aveena had no such concerns.

"Has Uncle Reg always been a kind generous man?" Aveena asked as they sat at a corner table.
"What a question, I'll have to think about it." Rosamund stirred her coffee even though there was no sugar in it. "I suppose really he has, he gives me everything I want, not what I need, what I want. We have a happy, comfortable life, we even went to Bermuda last year, but really I prefer France. I didn't tell him of course as it cost him a lot."
"What about me, I'm a stranger, he's only known our family for a short while and here you are buying me lovely clothes and uncle Reg paying for a Uni course which could change my whole life, that's not exactly normal is it?"
Rosamund took a drink from her cup before looking up at the young vibrant girl sitting in front of her.
"He seems to be a changed man since he retired. I have to admit that I was worried about his behaviour, going off in that big awful car of his, here, there and everywhere, taking silly pictures with that old Kodak Brownie of his and writing poems that he won't show me cause they're rubbish. But meeting you and your family seems to have calmed him down a bit. I think you fill a gap in our lives that Reg saw and I didn't. Perhaps he just had to find the missing piece to make us happy."
"I love my new clothes Aunt Rosamund, thank you so much."
Rosamund squoze her hand.
"Reg told me about losing your mum and now this business with your dad. Anything we can do to help, you just ask."
Aveena lent over and quickly kissed her on the cheek.
"Well that's a first. Shall we go home and watch the 'X' Factor?"
"Oh yes please! Dad hates it, says Simon Cowell is just a rich snail with a gold plated shell."
Rosamund rose up off the chair but Aveena sprang up.

It was getting dark as they pulled onto the drive, The red Jazz was parked at the top. Reg was asleep on the sofa, the opening of the front door woke him up.

"You two buy me anything?" He said, rubbing his eyes and yawning.

"No."

"Oh."

"Look at my new clothes Uncle Reg, aren't they fab!"

Reg's face lit up in a huge smile.

"Better have a fashion parade then before X factor comes on."

Aveena almost flew up the stairs. Reg looked at Rosamund, she was smiling too.

Monday morning was unseasonably wet and cold.

"Got everything? Your certificates, work, books, absolutely everything?"

"Yes Uncle Reg, I'm all organized."

"Yes, you'll have to be organized when you're in the Gobi desert trying to avoid the Gobi Death Worm."

"There's no such thing Uncle Reg and you know it. It's a myth."

"No it's not, it's a land descendant of the Lamprey eel, well actually they're fish, they bore into other fish and suck their blood. So the land version burrows underground, it can smell blood from five miles away, then it rears up and strikes like a giant leech sucking all your blood out within seconds. Nobody has ever lived that's why people don't believe it."

Aveena put her seat belt on looking very worried.

"After that it pupates, and later becomes a vulture."

Aveena slapped his arm.

"For goodness sake Uncle Reg, you had me really worried."

"Put some music on."

"What?"

"David Bowie, Hunky Dory."

It was as though the tyres cutting through the wet and the wipers squeaking were adding to the music. It was because she was with him. Reg sang along.

Will you stay in our lovers story,
If you stay, you won't be sorry,
Cause we believe in you,
Soon you'll grow,
So take a chance on a couple of Kooks
Hung up on romancing!

Reg forgot the next few words

And if the homework gets you down,
Then we'll throw it on the fire
And take the car downtown!

He laughed, looked at her and slapped her arm. Aveena hummed along, she knew the tune but not the words.

It wasn't 'Hogwarts' but it wasn't far off. Time eroded sandstone had different coloured sandstone around the ancient leaded windows. They opened with a brass latch with a screw stop. It wasn't polished. The office was academic darkwood, the patina of years giving it that 'book/learning' smell. The fifty something man in a dark grey suit but not a gown had goldwire bifocals and a secretary that sat at a desk between him and some filing cabinets. He checked Aveena's certificates and documents carefully and very slowly. Aveena fidgeted on an oak straight back chair. Fiddling with her hair as women do. Reg sat in a more comfortable old leather tub chair.

"So, you want to be a Vet Ms. Thomas?" His voice was consummate with his age declining into something that sounded like a croaking frog.
"Yes I do."
"Why?"
Aveena looked at Reg.
"I like animals."
The academic peered over his bifocals at Reg and Aveena.
"Rather a simplistic answer, don't you think?"
Aveena took a deep breath.
"I'm interested in the species of bear that inhabits regions of the Gobi desert in Mongolia. They're an endangered species and I would like to find out the reason they are in decline."
"That's more like it. The tuition fees are six thousand pounds a year Mr. ---------."
"Moorcroft." Reg filled in the pause.
"Mr. Moorcroft, we prefer the first year fee to be paid in advance. Accommodation and living costs are not our concern but we do have lists and support at the Students Union Office which is the next building down. How do you wish to pay?"
"Cash. She'll be living with us and I'll be responsible for her transport."
The man raised his eyebrows. Aveena glanced at Reg.
"I've just sold my car." Reg gave him the answer to his unspoken question.
"Please arrange that with my secretary Miss. Wilson, behind you."
The man looked at Aveena.

"The term starts on September the ninth, all new students should be in the University hall by ten in the morning." He dismissed them both with a gesture towards Miss. Wilson.

Reg took out the notes from his small black backpack. Miss Wilson looked at them and counted them very carefully before putting them in an envelope, putting the envelope in a green safe and giving Reg a small pink receipt. After that she turned to Aveena for her details. Miss Wilson was heading for forty but it could have been fifty, her clothes were 'functional', her face, pleasant but unhappy. Her hair, short, straight, almost boyish.She looked as though she'd been in the office a long time and would die there.

"Coffee?" Reg suggested as they walked back toward the car.
"Oh yes please, I need one after that." Reg had to speed up to keep up with her.

They sat on high uncomfortable stools at a bar whilst a super cool young male 'barista' drew pictures in froth. Aveena's was a heart, Reg's was an apple.

"Doesn't really encourage you to linger, tarry a while, does it?" Reg said.
"It's OK, the guy is quite dishy."
"Hadn't noticed." Reg commented whilst destroying his picture with a spoon.
"You never mentioned anything about living with you and Aunty Rosamund."
Reg looked at her.
"It's the cheapest option, student accommodation is always expensive and awful."
"What about the transport?"
"Aveena, consider me a taxi. Besides what else have I got to do? You'll probably only do about two or three days a week, the rest is down to you, library's, internet, that sort of thing. What they want from you is quick, accurate work; a lot of it."
"Thanks Uncle Reg." She put her hand on his for a moment. "I can't believe this is really happening."
Reg looked at her, she looked so much like her mother. A frozen face indelibly printed on his memory.
"Home tomorrow." Reg said.
"Yes, can't wait to tell dad all about it. Your lovely house, the chicken in your shed, our shopping trip, my new clothes, the university, Bristol, I've never been to Bristol before it looks lovely."

"Put some music on."
"What?"
"You choose."

Whitney Houston exploded out of the small speakers.

"The greatest love of all. I love that song." Reg muttered.

I believe the children are our future
Teach them well and let them lead the way
Show them all the beauty they possess inside
Give them a sense of pride to make it easier
Let the children's laughter remind us how we used to be.

Reg and Aveena sang along. It had stopped raining and the sun was peeing through. Leo Thrust was dead and Reg had moved on from the Lotus.

"Hello you two. How'd it go?" Rosamund was cooking in the kitchen. Sophia rubbed against Aveena's legs and then Reg's.
"All good Aunty Rosamund. You're now looking at a bona-fide student. I can officially stop washing and cleaning my teeth, start spitting, smoking pot and swearing after every other word."
"Oh dear, can't you have your tea before you start?"
"What is it?"
"Shepherds pie."
"Yes."

The evening was spent with Rosamund and Aveena chatting about everything and Reg dozing in front of the TV.

"Well! Thanks for absolutely everything Aunty Rosamund, the clothes, the food, the friendship, the kindness, everything."
Rosamund gave Aveena a long hug on the front doorstep. Reg was already in the car.
"Come again soon, come down for a week before you start Uni. It's been lovely having someone young to talk to. As you can see Reg is not a great conversationalist."
Rosamund and Aveena giggled.
"I will, I will. Promise." Aveena kissed her on the cheek then broke away, moving with ease towards the little red car. As she got in she waved and blew a kiss to her. It was raining again, but not heavily. It felt as though it would clear up. Reg backed down the drive. Aveena waved as they drove off.

Aveena's mood reflected the darkening weather as they travelled north, the elation and excitement of the weekend dissipated as her thoughts turned to her dad. The loss of her mother was terrible and now this.

Reg sank into silence, hiding behind a screen of concentration. He was trying his best to make amends, to help, to give her every opportunity he could but behind it all was Kathleen Thomas, the exploding watermelon and the gun.

"Shall I put some music on Uncle Reg?"
"No, I'm not in the mood."
"OK."

Aveena left Reg to collect up all her shopping and bags as she fled from his car and in through the front door of the house. When he got in, her arms were wrapped around her father.

"I've had such a great time dad, I've got a place at Bristol Uni, start early September. Aunty Rosamund has bought me loads of new clothes and uncle Reg has paid the fees for me. It's like a dream. I'm sure I'm going to wake up any minute now."

David Thomas was beaming at the sheer happiness of his daughter.

"Yes, well, you'd better put the kettle on and make a cup of tea for us all, Reg must be tired after that journey."

Aveena broke away and skipped into the kitchen.

"Well don't just stand there Reg, put the bags down and take a seat. Vanessa will be back soon, she's gone shopping." Reg noticed there was a walking stick within reach of David's chair.

"I've changed my car David, Rosamund hated my old one, refused to go in it. Got a little Honda Jazz, it's a great little car but tiring on a long run, in my old Vauxhall I'd hardly notice a journey like this but this one bounces you around whilst the engine buzzes in your ears. Rosamund likes it though."

"David grinned at him. *'The things you do for love.'* Ay Reg?"
"10cc, nineteen seventy-six,

Like walking in the rain and the snow

When there's nowhere to go
And you're feelin' like a part of you is dying
And you're looking for the answer in her eyes

Great song David, great song."

Aveena brought the tea through on a tray at the same time as Vanessa walked through the front door.

"Hey! Good timing! Hello Reg, you stopping to eat? Belly pork, roast spuds, carrots, peas and some stuffing."
"Now you can't turn that down Reg." Said David.
"No I can't. Better walk up to Threshers and buy a bottle."
"Sit down Reg, drink your tea, relax, tell me all about Bristol Uni."
Reg found it difficult to relax without some alcohol.

It was an almost noisy meal, Aveena tried a small glass of wine which made her even more ebullient and talkative, if that was possible? Vanessa's cooking was perfect and you could hardly tell David was ill. Reg felt at home, part of something, welcomed. Although Rosamund was lovely he always felt he was being watched, had to conform to her behaviour. They'd never talked about it but she was most definitely the dominant partner. Reg slept in the small spare room. Vanessa went back to her house at night, it was only around the corner so she walked. The chap next door kept pigeons, their gentle cooing was soothing. He looked up at the ceiling thinking that there should be another person in the house and not him. Eventually he went to sleep.

The morning was the same as yesterday evening, dull, overcast, quite chilly. Vanessa cooked him scrambled eggs on toast, he slipped her a hundred quid under the table.

"I'm leaving a tip for the board and lodging." Reg said to David as he slipped on his car coat and put a few notes on the small shelf by the telephone in the hall.
"Don't be silly. You're more than welcome anytime, after all you've done for this family it's the least I can do"
Reg thought about his last words, 'after all you've done for this family.' 'Yeah like kill your wife and Aveena's mother.' Reg thought.
"See you in about three weeks David. Rosamund would like Aveena to come down for a week before she starts uni, they get on like a house on fire. I've no idea what they talk about all the time."

"It's just women Reg, they're a mystery, Kathleen and Vanessa would talk for hours, non stop, then I'd ask what they'd talked about and she'd say 'oh nothing'. They've got different brains to us. Bye, have a safe trip."

"Bye, don't forget David, any problems call me."

"Will do."

Reg left pulling the door to behind him. Somehow the little car now seemed hollow and empty.

Twenty minutes of Radio two and congested early morning roads saw Bill Withers croon out of the speakers.

Ain't no sunshine when she's gone
It's not warm when she's away,

Reg hit the 'off' button then told himself he was stupid and clicked it back on again.

Ain't no sunshine when she's gone
And she's always gone too long
Anytime she goes away .

They should have tried harder, gone for tests, had some treatment, or even adopted. The car still smelt of her. Still in three weeks she'd be coming down to stay. He could pretend he was a normal dad. A bank, a taxi, talk to her, make sure she had everything she needed. Yes, it would soon go.

Then I look at you
And the world's alright with me
Just one look at you
And I know it's gonna be
A lovely day (lovely day, lovely day, lovely day, lovely day).

Shit! He'd missed the turn off. Never mind he'd head for the Derbyshire Dales, they were lovely this time of year. He missed Leo Thrust and the Lotus; he wasn't sure if Reg Moorcroft could write poems, even really bad poems. Nobody ever looked at Reg Moorcroft.

"You going off tomorrow?" Rosamund asked as casually as possible from her end of the sofa whilst he was watching 'Last of'.

"No, it's no fun in the Jazz, too buzzy busy and tiring, anyway I want to paint the spare room ready for Aveena."

"Reg?"

"What?"

Rosamund looked worried.

"It's nothing --------------- problematical is it?"

"Reg turned towards her."

"What are you talking about Rosamund?"

There was a pause, once she introduced her doubt, everything would change.

"Nothing, just thinking maybe it was a mistake to get rid of your Vauxhall, it seemed to make you happy and I've noticed you never wear your new clothes since you got the Jazz."

"No, it wasn't a mistake, you didn't like it, or my new clothes, so they had to go."

"I quite liked your new clothes."

"You never said." Reg turned back to the TV.

"What colour?" She asked.

"I thought a nice pale lilac."

"That sounds nice." Rosamund left the room to wash the dishes, she didn't like Last of The Summer Wine, far too childish, she could see why it appealed to men.

Everything was spick and span, lawns were cut, verges were weeded, drive swept, garage door washed, windows cleaned. Both Rosamund and Reg were looking forward to their 'lodger'. David had offered to pay some money towards her keep but Reg had refused.

"Shall I come with you tomorrow?" Rosamund asked.

"If you want, it's a long way, more than four hours in the Jazz."

"How long would it have been in a Lotus Carlton?" For the first time Rosamund revealed her hand, her awareness of the big car.

"Three hours and a speeding ticket." Reg grinned.

"Have you ever had a speeding ticket Reg?"

"No, I had a train ticket once, and when I was young I had some bus tickets."

Rosamund threw the Sunday Times supplement at him.

"Think I'll give it a miss, sounds too tedious plus I don't like your music."

"It's better than Doris Day or Matt Monro."

"I like them, they relax me."

"You can't relax in a Jazz, it's really a vibrator on wheels."

"Don't be disgusting."

Reg woke up and thought about what to wear. He'd wear his jeans and red shirt but just put his leather jacket in the car. He wouldn't wear his hat, it just didn't go. He'd be warm enough with just a sleeveless vest underneath. He'd wear the black Nike trainers he'd bought for speed walking. He lay in bed with his arms underneath the back of his head and decided he'd start speed walking again, he felt a lot better for it, even when it rained. He wondered what Rosamund was really going to say last night. He suspected that she suspected that there was something untowards going on regarding his feelings towards Aveena, but there wasn't. Yes she was a surrogate daughter and that was OK, but there was nothing else, he just liked marvelling at her youth, her enthusiasm and energy for everything. He loved the quickness of her movements, the flash of her eyes, the flick of her hair, when she was around, the world seemed a better place.

The long journeys now seemed tedious. The comfort break stops more frequent, just to break that tedium, he did, however, use the toilet at each stop. The rain was intermittent, he was even bored with all his cassettes. He'd stop and buy a new one.

A hot chocolate and chocolate muffin came to nearly two pounds. The chocolate wasn't all that hot and the muffin was stale. Captive audience, take it or leave it, we don't really care was the message coming through the scruffy wall loud and clear. Simon and Garfunkels greatest hits, four pound ninety nine. That looked good. He'd have to turn the volume up quite loud to drown out the buzzing engine.

Hello darkness my old friend,
I've come to talk with you again.
--------------------------------------,
The sound of silence.

Reg chuckled to himself, - wouldn't get much silence in this tin can - God he missed the Lotus. He could wear his cap in the Lotus.

By now, everybody at number sixteen knew Reg's knock at the front door, rat ta ta tat tat, tat tat.
"Come in Reg, it's not locked." David's voice shouted from the lounge.
"Is my passenger ready?" Reg said in a loud voice from the foot of the stairs.
"Just doing my hair Uncle Reg, won't be long." A young clear voice floated down the stairs.
"Stay for lunch Reg, Vanessa's gone to the chippy, cod, chips and mushy peas, now you can't say no to that can you?"

"No I can't David. How are you?"

"Have felt better Reg, have felt better." David was now in a wheelchair, his right leg visibly shaking. "You will look after her Reg won't you?"

Reg looked at David.

"Like she was my own David, like she was my own. You're every lucky man David Thomas, a very lucky man."

"I don't feel very lucky Reg, I have to admit."

"You have a beautiful young daughter who loves you to bits, I don't."

"Yes, I suppose you're right."

Vanessa came in the front door.

"Anybody for cod and chips?"

"Me please." Reg put up his hand like a school boy.

"Me please." David echoed, but he didn't put up his hand.

Aveena bounced down the stairs three steps at a time.

"Smells yummy aunty Ness. Lot's of vinegar for me."

Aveena was wearing light blue jeans and a tight knitted top that stopped short of her midriff. David looked at her.

"You'll need to wear something over that, you'll be cold."

"I'll be fine dad, it's summer."

"Ne're cast a clout til June is out. - you know the old saying."

"I'm not old dad, I'm young, I don't feel the cold."

David rolled his eyes towards Reg.

"You can't tell them anything Reg, they never listen."

"Maybe we were the same at that age David?"

David smiled.

"Maybe."

Eating the fish and chips together was just matter of fact. He wasn't a guest anymore, he was part of their world. Aveena hugged her father for a long time, tears streamed down both of their faces. Vanessa gave a family hug to Aveena and a polite hug to Reg. He slipped her some notes as she did so.

"Safe journey you two." Vanessa said, standing at the front door and waving.

"Which way we going Uncle Reg?"

"Thought we might stop off for a Bakewell tart and a mug of tea."

"Where?"

"Bakewell."

"Groovy. I've got a new cassette for the journey."

"What is it?"

"New Kids on the block."

"Oh! Don't think I know any of the words to any of their songs."

Aveena ignored him, kicked off her pumps and put her feet up on the dash.

It was five thirty when they arrived. Reg automatically scanned the house as he drove onto the drive. It looked nice in the warm evening sun, he'd have to cut back the bamboo, it was blocking out the light to the front door. Somebody had given him a small bush of it at work and it had grown like billio!

Rosamund had heard the car and was standing at the door.

"Hello you, It's so good to see you, I'm so excited having you here to live for a while, we can really get to know each other properly and have lots of chats." Rosamund gave Aveena a big hug. "Come on in, Reg will bring your stuff."

Reg looked up at Rosamund, but they'd already gone inside. He opened the tailgate and brought in all her bags.

"What's for tea?" Reg asked, putting down her bags in the hall. Aveena was fussing over Sophia. Rosamund was fussing in the kitchen.

"Poached eggs on toast with mushrooms, Did your dad like your new clothes?" Reg had been summarily dismissed, girl gossip was far more important.

"What you doing Uncle Reg?" Her face appeared at his shed door, her skin was clear and smooth, time had yet to find her. Reg pushed the door further open.

"Come in if you want, this is the nerve centre of the UK Nuclear Weapons establishment."

"Looks like a garden shed to me." She giggled.

"Don't let the ----------------------------- too late." Molly the chicken scooted past their legs and fluttered up onto the rag pile.

"What a beautiful chicken," Aveena put out her hand to stroke it but withdrew it quickly when Molly tried to peck her.

"It's not a beautiful chicken, it's a dinosaur disguised as a chicken. Did you know that dinosaurs are the direct descendants of birds, no, it's the other way round, birds are the direct descendants of dinosaurs."

"You're having me on uncle Reg."

"No I'm not, some of the smaller dinosaurs grew feathers, not to fly but to keep warm, then they found that they were useful for hopping about which of course developed into flight. You should know this being a Mammalogist."

"That's the study of mammals Uncle Reg, the study of birds is ornithology and the study of dinosaurs is Paleontology."

"Of course, I knew that. Just testing. Now in answer to your question, I started out to clean and sharpen the blades of the mower, but that progressed to sharpening this 'Billy hook' which I intend to use on the bamboo plant in the front garden."

"What about Molly?"

"She's in love with me, but we have this 'understanding'."

Aveena laughed as Reg tried to shooo Molly out of his shed. He loved to hear Aveena laugh.

Their house was now a home for three people. It lit up when she was there. Rosamund and Aveena did everything together, Reg did everything else that Rosamund told him to do and everything that Aveena wanted him to do. It was a happy place filled with laughter, jokes and peaceful contentment. She was the daughter they'd never had, the daughter they always wanted. Rosamunds dark thoughts and worries disappeared as time went by.

"Have you got absolutely everything for tomorrow?" Reg asked Aveena from the corner of the sofa whilst watching Emmerdale.

"Yes Uncle Reg, I'm all organised."

"She's all organised Reg, has been for days, she's not like you." Rosamund chipped in.

"How's your dad?"

"Not good, they had a commode delivered yesterday. He sleeps downstairs now."

Reg didn't really know what to say so he just said 'Ummmmmm.'

The run down the Wye Valley was always beautiful. Not always straightforward, there was always some bit of road collapsing, some flood damage or a tree down, so often there were diversions. But when there wasn't and when Tintern Abbey came into view through an early morning grey mist, it was magical. Made even more so because the girl sitting beside him was pure, untainted by the cuts and bruises of life. Still assuming that what she wanted she would get, her eyes didn't see any dangers or her vision ponder any problems. She was nervous, of course she was, that was all part of it, but that would disappear as she found her way around, became confident, made friends, laughed and sang in a pub. Reg usually taxied her two or three times a week, sometimes she stayed over with friends if she went out at night. Reg made sure she was never short of money. He loved to watch her hurry away from his car, her teenage youthful shape moving effortlessly, almost floating, her books, bags and everything flapping about in her wake. Then she'd be gone and he'd head for home. There was a point to his life. Rosamund was happy, it was as though Aveena and Rosamund fed off each other, it amazed him that they never stopped talking. He hadn't written a poem in ages. The time passed so quickly

Chapter 12.

"Well, there's good news and bad news boss." Rick O'Keefe said as he knocked and entered through the open office door.

Ken France sat behind his desk.the most important thing on it was a box of Kleenex tissues. He had a streaming cold and felt like shit. He should have stayed at home but dosed himself up and came in because the 'Underwood' file was required for court tomorrow. Terry Underwood was as sharp as his dad, maybe even sharper, rented a modest house in the country with his girlfriend, applied for a mortgage then when it was granted ran away with the cheque. Australia was the word on the street. They were going to hear the case in his absence. The branch manager of the Woolich had already been sacked. It was a mess.

"The good news, I need cheering up."
"The good news is that the forensic lab has found a DNA marker on a piece of that exploded watermelon that's been in the freezer for centuries."
"WaterMelon? What watermelon?"
"The one the offender blew to bits with a shooter in the Yorkshire Building Society office."
"Um! Yes, sorry, I'm with you now. And the bad news?"
"It comes back to one Reginald Geoffrey Moorcroft, date of birth the third of March nineteen twenty eight."
"Bit old to be a bank robber."
"Yes, it gets worse, the hit is down to the West Mercia Police Officer and Support Staff bank. Apparently he's a recently retired Crimes Analyst, blemish free, not even a speeding ticket, not even a parking ticket. Absolutely whiter that white Boss."
"What do you think Rick?" Ken sneezed three times. "Sorry Rick, shouldn't be here should I?"
"No, you should be at home in bed with something hot."

"Yeah I did call Spohia Loren but she was busy cooking." They both laughed.
"I think that this Moorcroft chap visited a supermarket somewhere and picked up, then rejected said watermelon."

Ken France blew his nose again and pondered.

"Sounds sensible, nevertheless technically he's a suspect to a robbery and possibly manslaughter. When you've got time, take someone with you, an aide will do, go down and sort it. You'll have to nick him, take him to the nearest local nick, interview and bail him, then get back to me."
"Do you think nicking him is necessary boss?"
"Have to, if it came out, we'd be criticized for not complying with P.A.C.E., you'll have to have his drum searched as well, expect the local 'woodentops' will help you there. No rush on this Rick, whenever you can squeeze it in."
"OK boss, will do. Why don't you go home before you infect the station."
"Yeah, I'm going to finish this file then admit defeat. Rick?"
"Yes boss?"
"The official line is that the North Yorkshire Police are of the opinion that the correct person was gaoled for this offence. In case anyone asks."
"Understood boss."

Chapter 13.

He loved Fridays, the traffic was a nightmare but it didn't matter. He'd wait for her at the bottom of Park Street. He'd see her coming in the mirror, laughing and skipping about with her new friends, hair, books and bags everywhere. The journey home would be music and chatter, Rosamund would have some plan for Saturday, they'd go off and Reg would stay at home, do a few 'bloke' things and wait for them to come home. Sunday was a relaxing, cooking day, then TV. Aveena would spend most of the afternoon on the phone to her dad. The phone bill was enormous but he never let her or Rosamund see it.

That was the sequence of events. It had become a happy routine.

"Everything packs up in about three weeks Uncle Reg for Christmas. Will you take me home or shall I get a train?"
"I'll take you of course, be good to see your dad and Vanessa again."
Rosamunds Beetle was parked at the top of the drive. He parked behind it on the slope. Reg pulled the handbrake up an extra notch and put it into gear just to be safe. Fifty yards down the road Reg had noticed a dark blue Cortina with two men in it. Sophia greeted them with a quick spray on the front left wheel before following them in through the unlocked front door hoping for food. Rosamund was in the kitchen.

"Ummmm! Smells good." Reg said depositing her bag and a carrier bag at the bottom of the stairs.
"Nothing special 'Spag Bol' with baked apples for pudding."
Reg moved to her side, peered in at the meat sauce, sniffed then licked the spoon, put out his left hand and pinched her bottom. Rosamund pretended to be offended, brushing him away."
"I saw that Uncle Reg. I'm going to call the police for assault!" She giggled and sprang up the stairs two steps at a time with her bags. The front door bell rang.

Reg broke away from Rosamunds side and opened the front door. There were two men standing in front of him. One was tall, thin and young with a long thin face and a moustache. The other was shorter, older, with a round congenial face but eyes that disbelieved before a word was spoken.

"Good evening." The shorter one said. "Are you Reginald Geoffrey Moorcroft?" The use of his full name set alarm bells ringing and his pulse soaring.
"Maybe, who's asking?"
"I'm Detective Sargeant Rick O'Keefe and this is Temporary Detective Constable Ian Davies from North Yorkshire Police." The two officers produced small black wallets with a badge and a card inside.
"May we come in?"
"Yes of course, what's this about Officers?" Reg was trying desperately to hide his panic. Trying to control his breathing and voice. He knew that someone who was a detective sargeant would be looking for signs, signs of panic, nervousness, fear. Something that would give him a clue of how to pitch his approach. Rosamund and Aveena were looking and listening. Reg closed the kitchen door.

"Please don't take this the wrong way Sir, but we have an anomaly we have to clear up. I'm sure it's a mistake, an unfortunate coincidence but it's something that has to be done, unfortunately since the Police and Criminal Evidence Act came in we have no option." O'Keefe's affable, round, disarming face and voice was starting to have a deceitful calming effect. "Reginald Geoffrey Moorcroft I'm arresting you on suspicion of aggravated armed robbery of the Richmond Branch of the Yorkshire Building Society and suspicion of manslaughter of one Kathleen Brenda Thomas. DC Davies please caution Mr. Moorcroft."

Rosamund Moorcroft and Aveena Thomas were listening behind the kitchen door. Rosamund went white and nearly collapsed. Aveena held her and sat her down at the kitchen table.

"What on earth's going on? Armed robbery, manslaughter? Who on earth is Kathleen Brenda Thomas?" Rosamund blurted out between sobs and tears.
"Kathleen Brenda Thomas is my mother." Aveena said it almost in a dream as her mind raced to make sense of it all. "She died in hospital after nine months of being in a coma, She'd gone into it after a heart attack. It's impossible for Uncle Reg to have had anything to do that. I'm sure this is all a terrible mistake." Aveena put her arm around the ashen faced Rosamund who was shaking in her seat.

Reg popped his smiling face around the kitchen door.

"Just got to go to the local nick for a while with these officers, help them with a few enquiries. My old job, you understand, won't be long, couple of hours."

"Shall I cuff him Sarge?" Davies asked his Sargeant.
"Certainly not." O'keefe pretended to admonish his subordinate with his voice, eyes and face. Reg picked up his car coat off the peg as he left the house with them. Not a word was said in the car.
Then they were gone. Rosamund and Aveena just looked at each other, Aveena burst into tears, the happy bubble of her life was bursting, Rosamund stood up and filled the kettle at the sink. Everything was familiar, the click of the kettle as she pushed down the switch, the ten seconds before the noise of the water heating began, the clink of the mugs, the packet of tea bags, the milk from the fridge. The discipline of the process, a distraction from the surreal reality of the last ten minutes.

The nearest 'nick' was three miles away in Wales. DC Davies struggled to find the 'backyard' but finally found it and a place to leave the car. Reg, Okeefe and Davies waited at the steel plated blue door. After three presses of the bell a bemused desk sargeant opened the door.

"And you are?"
"Just for interview Sarge, no need to book him in." O'Keefe produced his warrant card.
"Is he here voluntarily?"

There was a pause.

"Well technically he's under arrest." O'keefe admitted.
Can't do that, if he comes into my charge room, he gets booked in." O'keefe looked at Reg.
"Sorry!"

Reg had never been physically searched before. It was demeaning having some young man run his hands all over his body especially between his legs and his arse. The charge room smelt like all charge rooms, a mixture of fearful, sweat, false bravado, and Dettol. These days it was called a 'custody suite' It was painted cream, they all were.

"Interview room number one, just over there, tapes, labels and stuff on the table there." The desk Sargeant was most definitely Welsh and not too pleased with having to deal with a totally unexpected prisoner. "You will of course be searching his premises?" He asked.

"Actually Sarge, do you have a dedicated search team for that?" O'Keefe asked.

The dour sargeant looked up from the custody sheet.

"This is Wales boyo we don't have the money for things like that, the best I can do is offer you a couple of my shift boys. What exactly will they be looking for?"

"A large amount of cash and a gun, a revolver to be precise." DC. Davies chipped in.

Rosamund was not dealing well with the bomb that had just landed in her house. She sat on her end of the blue sofa shaking whilst Aveena brought her tea. There was no conversation, there was nothing to be said. It was as though without warning green men from mars had appeared and just vapourised her whole life. What possible explanation could Reg have for this. You don't get arrested for armed robbery and manslaughter for nothing and what was the connection with Aveena being here, living with them, loved by them both and her dead mother? She wanted to wake up from this nightmare, wanted to see Reg dozing in the chair, wanted to get his tea and moan at him for getting it down his shirt. She didn't want this. Couldn't cope with this. The front door bell rang. Aveena opened the door.

Two nervous, almost embarrassed young uniformed officers stood before her. At the bottom of the drive was a huge white Police transit van. One of the officers had a piece of paper in his hand.

"Hello, I'm really sorry but we have to conduct a search of your premises." Rosamund joined Aveena at the front door.

"What are you looking for?" Rosamund asked.

"A large amount of cash and a gun, a revolver."

"I can assure you, you won't find that here." Rosamund was becoming more composed by the minute as she tried to protect and salvage what was left of her normal life.

"This is a copy of the warrant madam, we'd prefer it if you remained present in each room as we look. To make it quicker quicker we could split up, you could assist me madam and the young lady could assist PC Knowles."

"Come in." Rosamund said.

The two police officers didn't want to do it. It was embarrassing, the house was obviously a respectable middle class house, not the usual filthy piss smelling dos hole they searched looking for drugs. PC's Jones and Knowles didn't try too hard, they tried not to make a mess, but every drawer was felt through, every cupboard looked in, every bed looked under, every mattress turned over. Rosamunds heart was breaking as these two men trashed their married life, their twenty three years together.

"What about outside?" PC.Jones asked Rosamund.
"Just a garden shed."
"Does it have a light in?"
"Yes."
"Better have a quick look, Roger you go, I'll stay here, don't be long."

Roger Knowles searched with his torch for a light switch. When he switched it on he was shocked. There sitting comfortably on top of a heap of rags was a chicken. She cocked her head and looked at him with one eye as chickens do. Roger smiled and went to stroke her, she pecked him twice making him pull his hand away and wipe the blood with his hankie. There was nothing of any interest in the small shed, just garden tools and boxes of 'come in handy' nuts, bolts and screws. The chicken stood up, ruffled her feathers then settled down again. Roger could see a clutch of eggs underneath her.

"Anything in the shed?"
"Yes, a vicious broody chicken." Roger displayed his wounded bloody hand.

"Thank you for your cooperation madam." The two PC's left Rosamund and Aveena with a crumpled piece of white paper and a shattered life. They looked at each other before hugging in tears.

"Aunty Rosamund, I want to go home, be with my dad, look after him, this was a mistake. Will you give me some money and get me a taxi to Hereford Station?"

The two women looked tearfully at each other. Rosamund took the young crying girl into her arms.

"No, go pack your bags, I'll take you there in the car, I'll stay a while if that's OK, help you with your dad, do a bit of cooking and cleaning. I'm good at that. I've no idea what's going on, not sure if I want to know. What I do know is that the trust in our marriage has gone and you can never get it back. I thought I knew Reg inside out, turns out I only knew 'the out', I'll never know 'the inside.'
"What about Sophia?" Aveena asked.
"Reg'll have to cope. Are you sure? What about your degree?"
"The Gobi bears can wait, dad can't."

Desk Sargeant Mike Hughes answered the crackling radio.

"Search teams have found nothing, you can go into interview now if you want.

"Please state your full name, address and date of birth." O'Keefe's soft lilting voice and friendly face made it easy. Maybe too easy.

"Reginald Geoffrey Moorcroft, Brookside, Old Trelawney Road, Whitechapple, Herefordshire, HR8 7QR. Third of March nineteen twenty eight."

"And what is your present occupation Mr. Moorcroft?"

"I'm retired."

"Retired from what?"

"I'm a retired Crimes Analyst based at Hereford Police Station."

"How long did you hold that position?"

"Eighteen years."

O'Keefe went to push back on his chair and stretch his legs but the chair was bolted to the floor. Davies sat against the wall but said nothing.

"You have been arrested on suspicion of armed robbery that occurred at the Richmond Branch of the Yorkshire Building Society on the afternoon of Tuesday the fifth of February nineteen eighty nine. Can you tell me all about it?"

Reg looked at him.

"I've no idea what you're talking about."

"Have you ever been to Richmond?"

"Yes."

"When?"

"I've no idea, a year, maybe eighteen months ago, soon after I retired."

"And why did you go there?"

"Write a poem."

O'Keefe glanced at Davies.

"You travelled all the way to Richmond in Yorkshire just to write a poem?"

"No."

"Go on."

"I also took a photo of the town sign, you know, the roadside sign with the name of the town on it."

"Why?"

"That's what I was doing at the time, at a bit of a loose end after I retired so I decided to visit places I'd never been to, take a photo and write a poem about each place"

"So you're a sort of 'travelling poet'?"

"Not really, just a tourist."

"And how did you travel?"

"In my car." Reg half lied.

"Did you spend the night in Richmond?"

"No, I moved on."

"Where to?"

"I can't remember."

"What did you do in Richmond?"

"Nothing, looked around, went into a military museum in a church, went into Sainsbury's, brought some sandwiches and fruit, sat on a bench in the square, ate my lunch, looked at people and wrote a poem."

"What fruit did you buy?"

"Good grief, what a question, as far as I can remember an apple and a banana."

"How about watermelons?"

"I did consider a watermelon as I like them but they wouldn't sell me a half one so I left it."

"Did you pick up any watermelons?" Reg looked at him bemused by his fascination with watermelons.

"Maybe, I can't remember, picking up a watermelon in Sainsburys is hardly a momentous event is it?"

"No, No." O'Keefe concurred.

"Have you still got the poem?"

"Yes."

"Where is it?"

"In my shed."

"In your shed?"

"Yes, it's in my shed in a tin box along with all the photos of the places I visited. The poems are on notelets stuck to the back of the photos."

"What's the tin box look like?"

"It's a rectangular flat box with a blue bird on the front."

"And whereabouts is it?"

"On the top shelf, on the left as you go in."

"Do you want me to radio up for a bobby to go and get it sarge?" Davies asked.

"No, we'll suspend the interview. I'll go and get it, you stay here with Mr. Moorcroft. Give me the car keys. I want to get a feel for Mr. Moorcrofts poetic shed." Detective Sargeant Rick O'Keefe smiled at Reg as he stood up.

"Hello again, sorry to bother you but I just need to get something from Mr. Moorcroft's shed. Sorry." Rick O'Keefe smiled at Rosamund as she let him in. By now she'd regained her composure.

"What's all this about Officer? You're aware that my husband was a very senior and respected member of the police support staff."

"Yes, we're aware of that, I'm sure it's all a huge mistake but since PACE came in we have no options anymore. Normally a thing like this would be bottomed out over a cup of tea and a chat but not these days, I'm sorry for all the upset."

"And what exactly is 'a thing like this'?"

"I'm afraid I can't disclose that."

"It's out the back. Go through the kitchen and out of the back door, mind the cat's litter tray."

"Thank you. Is there a light?"

"On your right as you go in."

The shift bobbies were right, there was a bloody chicken in there. As he put the light on she started furiously 'clucking', she tilted her head over to the right and gave him the evil stare with her left eye, then tilted her head over to the left and gave him another glare. Rick followed her gaze up to the top shelf, there was the tin, just as he'd said, top shelf, bluebird tin. Then he saw it, toward the back of the shed there was a small hole in the roof timbers. It had been sealed, covered over with a felt panel from the outside. Rick put up his hand, his little finger would just fit into it, the surrounding wood splinters all splayed outwards as though something small had passed through it at high speed.

"Thank you so much, once again I apologise for all this upset." His round congenial smiling face worked again.

"That's OK." Rosamund lied.

"Does he live in his shed?" O'keefe joked.

"Yes he only comes out for the toilet and food."

"How many years has he been living in it?"

"Oooh at least twenty." The beginnings of a smile came to her face.

Rick O'keefe sat in the car and opened the tin. There were dozens of black and white photographs of town name signs, each had a yellow notelet stuck to the back with a poem written in very small writing.

Richmond, here it was, no date though.

Richmondshire my dear,

Don't prick your finger in the market square,
Use the thimble to pray a prayer,
Pray Norman will keep his keep,
So we can lie in peaceful sleep,

The swirling Swale so washed and clean,
Falls swiftly in flood but is summer serene,
Picnics and ducks, sandwiches and children
The clean green grass, so sweet to sit on.

The market square, as big as you get,
If you can't buy it here then you don't need it yet,
People walk by, some plod, some skip
But most just trudge, no smile on their lips,

And here I am, a voyeur, a stranger,
Much better than being a visiting danger,
I can take time to look and know
Then disappear before the winter snow.

What the hell did that mean? '*Much better than being a visiting danger'.*

"Four fifty two, Sunday the twenty ninth of November nineteen ninety interview of Reginald Geoffrey Moorcroft resumed. I am showing Mr. Moorcroft a black and white photograph of the place name of Richmond Yorkshire on the back of which is affixed a yellow notelet on which is written a poem. Did you take this photo and write this poem?"
"Yes."
"When?"
"I can't remember, sometime last year." Reg lied.
"Can you explain this line of the poem - '*Much better than being a visiting danger,'*
What exactly did you mean by '*visiting danger'?*"
Nothing, it rhymed with '*stranger'.* I had a very fast car at the time and Richmond is such a sleepy old town. Maybe I was a danger, it's all I could think of that rhymed, as I said."
"I must inform you that there is forensic evidence that links you to the inside of the Richmond Branch of the Yorkshire Building Society. Can you explain that?"
"Maybe if you tell me what it is."

O'keefe paused, fiddling with his pen and deciding his next question.

"A D.N.A. marker has been identified on a piece or watermelon obtained at the scene of the crime."

"I wondered why you were asking about watermelons. Think I've already covered that."

"When did you visit Richmond?"

"I've already told you, sometime last year, I'm not sure exactly when. You've got my tin, you can see that I went to many places, took many photographs and wrote many poems. The poems are rubbish, I'll give you that, but writing rubbish poems is not a crime."

O'Keefe knew he was onto a loser. He snapped back.

"No but armed robbery is. I put it to you that you traveled to Richmond on Monday the twelfth of March nineteen eighty nine with the intention of carrying out an armed robbery at the Richmond Branch of the Yorkshire Building Society."

"Don't be ridiculous. I'm a retired Police Support Worker, an old man, I don't need money, why would I do a thing like that.?"

"Boredom." The previously silent DC Davies interjected. O'Keefe threw him a disparaging glance.

"Answer the question Mr. Moorcroft."

"The answer is no. Any more questions?"

O'keefe and Davies were silent for a while.

"Why is there a bullet hole in your shed roof?" O'keefe quietly asked.

The question came from nowhere and knocked him back. He could see O'Keefe noting the delay as he gathered his wits.

"It's not a bullet hole." Reg lied.

"What made it then?"

"I--I've no idea, I bought the shed in a farm sale, it was cheap 'cause there was damage to the roof, a hole, I fixed it with a felt patch on the outside." Reg almost visibly regained his confidence as he supplied a plausible answer.

"How long have you had the shed?"

"About five or six years."

"Where was the farm sale?"

"Shropshire somewhere, can't really remember."

"Seventeen twenty hours, interview concluded."

O'Keefe switched off the tapes and stood up.

"A few formalities Mr. Moorcroft then we'll drop you off at home. You'll be released on bail pending the conclusion of our enquiries."

Reg got out of the back door of the Cortina with his tin box and a green bail sheet. There were no lights on in the house. That was odd. Perhaps they'd gone out for a takeaway or something. Yes Rosamund wouldn't feel like cooking with all this going on. O'Keefe and Davies drove away as soon as he closed the door, not even a 'thankyou' or 'goodbye'.

"Are we going to stop somewhere for some food? Maybe a pint?" Ian asked.
"He bloody well did it. I know he did, every gut feeling I've got is telling me it was him." Rick O'Keefe thumped the steering wheel as they drove. "His wife joked that he'd lived in his shed for the last twenty years, yet he said he'd only had it for five years. Not a shred of evidence that would get passed the C.P.S. that hole in the shed roof was definitely a bullet hole, reckon he was messing with the gun and it went off."
"Do you reckon we should call in a search team sarge? You know, a proper search, may be run a detector over the garden just in case he's buried it."
"Naw, a bloke like that is far too clever, he'd have slung it one dark night into a very big river somewhere. He was a Crimes Analyst for Gods sake, he knows every trick in the book, but he did it alright. I'm not going to tell the boss, it'll upset him, he was a schoolmate of Hubby's so it's personal. Make sure your pocket book reflects that we found no conclusive evidence, sometime next week ask Diane to send a bail cancellation letter. "
"We didn't, here's a pub, let's stop."

The blue Beetle was heading north in almost sad silence as both women struggled with their thoughts. Sometimes a tissue was needed to wipe away moisture.

"My aunt Vanessa is Dad's carer at the moment, she's divorced, sometimes she stays the night if dad's not doing too well but usually she goes home, it's only round the corner, very convenient." Aveena was looking out of her window at the passing blackness dotted with lights.
"Your dad will think it's strange me turning up out of the blue."
"I'll tell him you're separated and needed to get away and very kindly offered to help with his caring. You being there will take the pressure off aunt Vanessa."
"You should write to the University, explain that your dad's seriously ill with Parkinsons and ask them if it's OK to come back after ---------------."

There was an awkward silence.

"After dad's died." Aveena added, staring straight ahead. The rumbling of the diesel engine was a panacea for the silence.

"What are you going to do aunt Rosamund?"
"No idea, Reg, my husband has become a total mystery to me. It's not really a marriage is it? You can't be best friends with half a person."

Reg unlocked the front door hiding the green bail sheet in his coat pocket as he went in. Sophia immediately appeared purring and rubbing against his legs, her tail rigidly upright. He called out but knew the house was empty. Putting the lights on he looked for a note, a message, but found nothing. He could manage poached eggs and beans on toast, he'd have that. Checking upstairs he found Aveena's room empty, her bed crumpled and untidy from last night, on it was a still damp towel, he smelt it, it smelt of her youth, her smile, her fun. He sat on the bed. If they'd left, then that was it, nothing more to be done, nothing to do, no one to give money to, no one to take here, there and everywhere, no one to make cups of tea for. Their bedroom was the same but things were missing, the red suitcase from the top of the wardrobe, the wardrobe doors were open, there were gaps where her clothes should be. The jewellry box was gone. Reg went down stairs and turned on the TV, he didn't know why, it was just habit, there was no one to sit on the other end of the sofa.

His prostate was getting worse, these days he had to go at least four times during the night. He couldn't sleep, Sophia jumped onto the bed beside him. She was taking advantage of Rosamund not being there, she never allowed Sophia on the bed. Reg stroked her and scratched between her ears, she liked that, stretching out and purring. He put the radio on, Gilbert O'Sullivan came out of the radio into the room

In a little while from now
If I'm not feeling any less sour
I promise myself to treat myself
And visit a nearby tower
And climbing to the top
Will throw myself off
In an effort to
Make it clear to whoever
Wants to know what it's like when you're shattered

Alone again, naturally!

Reg turned it off then got out of bed to go to the toilet. There was something wrong, his toilet habits were very regular, you could almost set your clock by them, seven thirty-ish every morning. The last few days he'd lost his appetite and he hadn't been, now, at five in the morning he had to go very quickly, evenso it was a strain, then it came, like a flood into the bowl, somehow it felt different.

He stood there in just his boxer shorts holding a bright red tissue in his hand staring into the red bowl. After five minutes, transfixed by the sight, he threw the tissue into the bowl and flushed everything away.

"Piles, that's what it will be." He clicked down the kettle and fed the cat.
The End.

Thoughts and comments to johnarthurcooper88@gmail.com

Printed in Great Britain
by Amazon

62809580R00092